The Mentor

by
Brian Rowe

Copyright © 2004 by Brian Rowe

All rights reserved. No part of this book shall be reproduced or transmitted in any form or by any means, electronic, mechanical, magnetic, photographic including photocopying, recording or by any information storage and retrieval system, without prior written permission of the publisher. No patent liability is assumed with respect to the use of the information contained herein. Although every precaution has been taken in the preparation of this book, the publisher and author assume no responsibility for errors or omissions. Neither is any liability assumed for damages resulting from the use of the information contained herein.

This is a work of fiction. Names, characters, places, and incidents either are the product of the author's imagination or are used fictitiously. Any resemblance to actual events or locales or persons, living or dead, is entirely coincidental.

ISBN 0-7414-2291-3

Published by:

INFINITY
PUBLISHING.COM

1094 New DeHaven Street, Suite 100
West Conshohocken, PA 19428-2713
Info@buybooksontheweb.com
www.buybooksontheweb.com
Toll-free (877) BUY BOOK
Local Phone (610) 941-9999
Fax (610) 941-9959

Printed in the United States of America
Printed on Recycled Paper
Published November 2004

I would like to dedicate this book to Ed and Delores McCalip of Holmesville, MS; to all Clinton, Mississippi School District bus drivers; to Jeff Polk of Palestine, TX; to Adam Stewerf, Ben Gray, Marchie Garcia, Larry Parcher, Alex Galvan, and Debbie Shier, living in different parts of southern California; and last, but certainly not least, all of the Delta blues players who have remained in poverty and obscurity.

Acknowledgments

I could not have written this book without the help of my family and friends, the first of whom is my wife, Nancy. Due to my illiteracy with computers, Nancy and her mother, Pat Jordan, came to my rescue; her father, Walter Jordan, advised me in his apperception of life on the farm; my cousin Cherrie Kilby lent her knowledge of feminine apparel from the early seventies; my sister, Becky McNair, who adroitly illustrated the book's cover; my friend, Alex Galvan, provided his expertise in the musical realm. I accept responsibility for all of the uncorrected mistakes and poor choice of words. This book is a work of fiction.

Foreword

The sole intellect of man may prove divisive, but that which touches the heart and soul unifies. Well, there ends my attempt to be a writer and philosopher. However, what follows is a heart-warming tale of a gentleman who in his pursuit of perfection within his art form, endears himself to those who possess a God-given ability to move people in ways that can only be described as far-reaching: a reach that crosses cultural and physical barriers, a reach that continues to this day. Within this touching story about people with diverse heritages and life experiences, one becomes engulfed with the "soul" objective and cannot help to be enthralled with how the objective is realized and the peripheral events along life's path which help to define its outcome. "…but that which touches the heart and soul unifies." Certainly, this was borne out of what Mr. Rowe has beautifully shared, and you will soon experience after page 1.

Alex Galvan
Professor of Music
Citrus College
Glendora, California

Introduction

First came the musicians in …
REMOTE PARTS OF WEST AFRICA

Then came…
THE MISSISSIPPI DELTA BLUES PLAYERS

Then came…
ELVIS

Then came…
THE BRITISH INVASION

Then came…
THE SEVENTIES

One

London, England—1973
Chief Editor's Office for *Electric Guitar*, Britain's leading rock and roll magazine.

MICK DAVIES, CHIEF EDITOR for *Electric Guitar*, was desperate for a stimulating article. Sales had declined, and he was beginning to feel the pressure from his usually patient employer. Increased revenue prompted increased bonuses, but a dip in sales almost always brought a quick visit from the president to Mick's office. In the magazine's twelve years of existence, things had never been this drastic. The buck stopped at Mick's desk, and he knew it. Changes had to be made soon. Pondering what he could do to boost earnings—and to hold on to his job--Mick decided he would risk it all with a fledgling reporter whom he had recently hired. He paged Roger Jensen into his office.

"Yes, Mr. Davies?"

"Good morning, Roger. Have a seat, won't you? You have been with us for how long now?"

"Three weeks," Roger answered, as he sat in front of Mick's desk.

"Three weeks. Well, I have a rather unique assignment for you."

"Oh?"

Mick, a chain smoker, paused while he looked for a place to extinguish his cigarette in his congested, glass ashtray. "Yes. Once a year, for ten years, I have asked Ian Smythe for an interview. And every year he has declined. I want you to call him."

"Me? Do you think that is such a good idea for a novice such as I to interview Britain's most celebrated rock and roll star?"

"Maybe. About ten years ago, we ran an article on Ian and his band. Let's just say that our reporter stretched the truth about Ian, and he has never forgotten it. Ian Smythe may seem like just another rock and roll star to many, Roger, but he *does* believe in accurate reporting. Because of that article ten years ago, he has since rejected all of our interview requests. I've been told he has also rejected everyone else's requests as well. Kind of a recluse, you know."

"What makes you think he will change his mind now?"

"I don't. But it is worth a try." Mick had not hinted to any of his subordinates the financial straits of the magazine. Roger, especially, was totally unaware of Mick's ulterior motive for the interview. While

Mick had wanted to do an article with Ian for the last decade, there could not have been a more ideal time for it than now. The magazine might have to fold if there wasn't a turnaround soon. Mick felt that a great story on one of the greatest rock and roll musicians of the era could be just the spark that they needed. The enigma surrounding the British hermit would only help matters because no one else had been successful in interviewing Ian, either.

"All right, if you prefer."

Twenty minutes later, Roger re-entered Mick's office.

"Yes?" asked Mick.

"Ian said he would do the interview."

"Well, what do you know! I wonder, what made him change his mind?"

Roger shrugged his shoulders. "I did not speak with him personally. A female—a paramour, I presume--answered. When I told her I was a reporter with *Electric Guitar*, she turned to ask Ian. He said he would do it."

"Great! When is it scheduled?"

"Tomorrow."

"Tomorrow? I had planned for you to do a story on Trower tomorrow." Pausing, Mick then advised, "Never mind; I will get Elizabeth to cover that story. *You* drive to Cambridge."

THE NEXT MORNING Roger traveled the one hundred kilometers north to Cambridge. Roger Jensen was a young, energetic cum laude graduate of The London School for Journalism. He had interviewed with the *London Globe* as a senior, anticipating a career with the illustrious paper. But Roger never heard back from them. A neophyte newspaper on the outskirts of London had offered Roger a volunteer position as a photographer, which he politely refused. He was looking forward to his appointment with the *London Daily* in two weeks.

However, Mick Davies was desperately in need of a reporter. *Electric Guitar's* employee turnover ratio had always been exceptionally high. A *Globe* associate whom Mick knew passed Roger's job application on to Mick.

Roger had always dreamed of being a journalist for one of London's largest newspapers or magazines. His parents had tried unsuccessfully to discourage him from that field because newspapers' remuneration for a recent graduate was meager to say the least.

Furthermore, Roger was somewhat indifferent to rock and roll. When Mick originally notified Roger of a vacancy, he immediately declined, explaining that he wasn't interested in narrowing his writing skills to one topic. Rock and roll simply had no appealing value to Roger; he preferred English folk music. But when the major newspapers' jobs went to friends of employees, Roger felt he had no choice but to call Mick and set up an interview for the position.

Mick's hands were tied as well. Journalistic experience and adoration for rock and roll music were his preferences, but not mandatory requirements for the vacant reporter's position. Anyway, Mick's employer was pressuring him to hire another journalist due to the dismissal of yet another the week before.

Making his way down Ian's winding driveway, Roger soon found himself in an agricultural setting. The first observation Roger made was of several corroded, antique farm implements. An old plow with a broken handle sat over to the right side. Nearby was an old, rusty tractor missing half of its seat. On the left of the meandering driveway lay a fertilizer hopper, a middle buster, a cultivator, and two turning plows. As he drove on, Roger passed a two-story barn made of cypress wood. Adjacent to the barn, Roger noticed a corral, and inside stood two strawberry roan mules staring at the car and its driver.

A middle-aged man dressed in dirty overalls with a large straw hat was exiting the barn, carrying a bale of hay. The man looked Roger's way and waved.

A rustic shanty next caught Roger's eye. Why is *that* building here? Had he made a wrong turn? Roger stopped his car and gazed at the small, plain, two-room shack. Roger observed a tin washtub, its bottom rusting out, hanging on the house's side. All sorts of primitive tools were lying about. Underneath the front eave of the house lay a wooden water trough. The porch's single window was missing two of its glass panes. The dirty screen door stood partially ajar in the middle of the porch. Roger eyed an old butter churn nearby. The house's siding consisted of old, unpainted pine boards. Roger noticed a deteriorated vent pipe extending from the roof.

To Roger, all of this seemed odd for a rock and roll star to possess. But Mick had warned Roger to be prepared for the unusual; he just didn't specify in what way. As Roger continued to drive down the private road, he eventually came to Ian's home. He was awed by the splendor surrounding the rock star's two-story castle. Roger was quite perplexed by the transition from a pastoral scene to a luxurious estate.

Roger exited the car and knocked on the massive, wooden front door. His dad was a furniture maker, so Roger was instinctively drawn to the door's outstanding craftsmanship. Suddenly, Roger saw the man with the straw hat exiting from the barn and riding one of the mules around the side of the castle.

"Mr. Jensen?" asked the elderly, black butler who was dressed in a white dinner jacket and black slacks.

"Yes. I have an appointment to interview Mr. Smythe."

"Come in, Mr. Jensen. Mr. Smythe is in the parlor to the right." Roger handed him his coat. The foyer held some of the finest nineteenth century antique furniture Roger had ever viewed. For a brief second, Roger thought it strange for Ian to have a black butler, but he gave it no more consideration.

Upon entering the parlor Roger observed two women; the first, a young adolescent, was sprawled on a carved mahogany recamier. She wore cotton corduroy bellbottoms and an embroidered flower power blouse along with Dr. Scholls sandals. On a mahogany settee sat the other woman who was barefoot and appeared to be thirty-something. Roger assumed she was the teen's mother. She too was dressed in similar attire, wearing large, silver hoop earrings dangling from her lobes. Near the farthest corner from Roger stood a Petrof baby grand piano made of the finest rosewood and walnut.

There he was again, that pitifully-dressed man with the straw hat. He must be a hired servant, thought Roger. The man was of medium height and build, clean-shaven and sported a long ponytail. His pants were tucked into his black work boots. Roger assumed the man must have rushed in the mansion's back door to be in the parlor so quickly. But what was *he* doing in the parlor?

"Hello, I am Roger Jensen, with *Electric Guitar*."

"We have been expecting you. I am Ian Smythe," he replied as he removed his straw hat, revealing his long brown hair.

Roger quickly and inquisitively asked, "But aren't you the one I saw near the barn and also on the horse?"

"Yes, I am. But it's a mule, Mr. Jensen, not a horse."

Roger reached out to shake Ian's hand. The women remained seated, obviously expecting to be included in the interview.

"I almost called and cancelled your appointment, Mr. Jensen. I said that I would never give any more interviews, *especially* to *Electric Guitar*."

"Yes, I had heard."

The older of the two women rose from the settee. "Would you care for some sasparilla tea, Mr. Jensen?"

"No, thank you. Pardon me, but don't you mean *sar*saparilla?" Roger asked in a corrective tone.

"No," she calmly answered.

"Just what kind of article are you looking for?" asked Ian.

"Well," Roger began rather methodically, pen and paper in hand, "for the last ten years, yours is unquestionably the most popular British rock and roll band. Your songs consistently rise to the top of the heavy metal charts. Midnight's concerts are always sold out. The band's albums are always best sellers. Next to the queen, you may be the most popular citizen of the United Kingdom. Yet, the music industry had never heard of you or any other of Midnight's members until ten years ago. *Electric Guitar* would like to devote one entire issue—a special edition--to Midnight. If you don't mind me saying so, Mr. Smythe, your music is unlike any other British group. Without sounding *offensive*, Mr. Smythe, you seem to be quite eccentric."

"Without sounding *boastful*, Mr. Jensen, many things are unique about me. For example, how many other Englishmen have black butlers? Another thing, had you visited here in the summer, you would have seen a large vegetable garden on the side of my castle. Do you know who tends to my garden, Mr. Jensen? I do. And, no doubt, you have observed my clothes. Right, Mr. Jensen?"

Before leaving London, Roger had rehearsed with Mick the scripted questions. Mick wanted to be certain that provocative, yet inoffensive, questions were raised. "But, while other British bands have written and played many good tunes, Midnight surpasses them all in originality and quality. Therefore, what do you attribute to this? Many of our readers would love to know what influenced Midnight to include the harmonica, the fife, the piano, and the panpipes so frequently in their songs."

Ian dragged on an extra-long cigarette before replying. "Well, Mr. Jensen, I will tell you what has influenced me more than anything else—provided your article is written like I tell you. I do not want to read inaccuracies in your magazine. If I do, I will be contacting my attorneys. Agreed?"

"Yes, absolutely, Mr. Smythe. Absolutely."

"Well, Mr. Jensen, I will give you your article. Again, you must report it as you are told. I may not be chosen as the next bishop of London, but *at least* I speak the truth. I detest lies and liars. There is a reason, Mr. Jensen, you nor anyone else had heard of Midnight's members before ten years ago. It is because we had just started. Peter, Colin, Niles, and I were all fledgling musicians from Cambridge. Before we began to play together as a band, I was introduced to the blues. Are you familiar with blues music, Mr. Jensen?"

"Somewhat, Mr. Smythe. Admittedly, I haven't thoroughly researched it. Didn't blues originate in the city of Memphis, in the States? Or, was it Chicago? If I'm not mistaken, Muddy Waters is from Memphis." Ian glanced at the two women. Roger wanted to make Mick happy, so he pretended to know about the blues in order to impress Ian. However, his feigning fooled no one in the room, not even the teenage girl.

"Memphis and Chicago *are* two popular cities in the States for blues," Ian replied. "St. Louis and Detroit are two more. However, Mr. Jensen, the blues did not originate there. And McKinley Morganfield— a.k.a. Muddy Waters--is not from Memphis.

"You see, Mr. Jensen, in the early fifties, some of the more popular blues musicians were invited to England. Not only Muddy Waters, but Lead Belly, Lonnie Johnson, Big Bill Broonzy, and a few other musicians visited England. They were an immediate hit. I suppose you are too young to remember them. At any rate, in 1956, I was privileged to hear a few of these blues players because my father worked for a local radio station. As I began to listen to these blues musicians, I found myself obsessed with their style of music. It is rather difficult to explain, really. At the time, I knew little about it. I was already a decent pianist. But I felt I had to learn more.

"Some of Britain's top rock and roll bands---Cream, Zeppelin, the Stones—were later influenced by these black blues musicians. I decided then that I wanted to be a blues musician. I felt that the best way for me to learn more about the blues was to travel to America. After all, what better way to learn something of which one knows little than to go to the source? That is more or less what a reporter's job entails. Right, Mr. Jensen? I suppose if it is as you say, that Midnight is England's best rock and roll band, it is partly due to the commitment I made when I decided to travel to the States.

"You see, Mr. Jensen, my father had been asked if he would drive some of these blues players to a concert hall where they would be playing that night. He asked me if I wanted to go. Of course, I did not want to miss this opportunity. I especially remember one statement that was made in the car as we were taking the men to their concert. My father asked one of the men why he thought the British could not satisfactorily duplicate their blues singing. The reply was, 'It take a man that *have* the blues to *sing* the blues.' I never forgot that, Mr. Jensen. In other words, Britain's best bands were asking these black men to come to England; likewise, some members of these British bands visited the States as well. But something was still missing; there was an enigma that existed with these Delta musicians. We still were not able to sing with the same feeling as these blues men had instinctively done.

"I felt I should visit the States to see if there was something else that could be done in order to get the feel of a blues man. So in 1959, I borrowed money from my wealthy aunt in Cardiff and traveled to the States, first to Memphis. As I visited the Bealle Street area of Memphis, I began to ask around. I even had a couple of drinks at the Monarch with the legendary blues man, Fred Robinson. From there, my inquiries led me to what is called the Delta in the neighboring state of Mississippi. There is where it began for me, Mr. Jensen. In the Delta. I cannot take full credit for Midnight's music. Yes, I have written most of the songs that Midnight sings. But truthfully, Mr. Jensen, I was heavily influenced by the blues musicians of the Delta."

Two

Fourteen years earlier (1959)
Memphis Municipal Airport

NOTHING EXTRAORDINARY occurred on Pan Am Flight 912 from London's Heathrow to New York International Airport. It was Ian's first trip on a Boeing 707 jet; but when he was thirteen, he had flown on a Cessna 310 with his mother to Cardiff, Wales, to visit her sister.

Traffic flow was minimal that Thursday afternoon at New York International. There was a three-hour layover for Memphis-bound Flight 661. Although he was uneasy about napping at twenty thousand feet, Ian decided it was time to catch up on some sleep. Before he had settled comfortably in his waiting area chair, Ian overheard part of a conversation between two gentlemen sitting behind him. Their nasalized accents and jargon had Ian somewhat confused. Out of curiosity and boredom, Ian decided to eavesdrop.

"Nawh, my peas ain't ready yet. Yo'rn?" asked the one.

"Nawh, mine neithuh," replied the other.

"Wouldja' look a yonduh," said the one. "Is that a boy-ah o' a guhl?"

"I can't tay-el, not jest yet, leas' wise," replied the other. "But I read a mag-uh-zine ah-tuh-kel thah uhtah day when I wuz at Earl's bah-buh shop. Said that rock an' roll music's gone cause thah young men in this country to staht wearin' theah ha-uh long. I reckon that's one of 'em right theah. That's all we need, long-haired fellahs. Next thang ya' know, they'll be frat-uh-nizin' with thah col-uhd folks."

"Yep. Say, Taylor, whin's thah last time Bruthuh Jones got a raise from thah chu-uch?" asked the one.

"Don't r'call. Don't need one, does he?" Taylor asked.

"I ain't fur shore. All y'all on thah committee might want tah look at that ag'in. Jest givin' 'eem a bunch o' peas, squash, an' t'maters tah help 'eem along don't always git it."

"We payin' 'eem sixty-five dollahs a week. Ain't that enough, seein' as how we pay for thah pah-son-ege and thah util'ty bills an' stuff," asked Taylor in a rhetorical tone. "The Lord 'el take ca-eh o' 'eem an' his wife an' thim chillen'. B'sides, Willie Harper said that's what they pay theah preachuh ovuh at Calv'ry. What time is it, J. T.?"

"Three fifteen," replied J. T.

"Well, we fixin' tah be flyin' home pritty soon," Taylor commented.

"Yep, I'll be glad, too. I really don't like flyin' that much. Whin we git tah Memphis, I hope ow-ah wives are theah so we kin git back tah Little Rock soon. Can't wait tah sleep in m'own bed."

Ian's eyes closed, and his mind drifted off into oblivion. When he awoke, the two Southern gentlemen had disappeared. The last cant Ian remembered hearing from the pair was concerning the destruction a tornado had caused in Jonesboro.

"Last call for Flight 661 to Memphis, Tennessee."

Ian scurried to the attendant and gave her his ticket, only to find that he had been assigned a seat in the back of the plane. As he walked down the plane's aisle, Ian heard the two men's voices again. Although Ian had not seen their faces until then, there could be no mistaking their inflection. Both appeared to be in their early sixties with greased-back gray hair, paunches, and glasses. Twins, perhaps, thought Ian. Little did the pair know that another passenger knew how much Brother Jones' weekly church stipend was.

After landing in Memphis, Ian eventually made his way to luggage pick-up and grabbed his brown bundled suitcase. Two things quickly came to Ian's attention when he first stepped outside of the terminal. One, there were less available taxis than in London; and the other, his long-sleeve, cotton chambray shirt with French cuffs and his Lee Rider jeans were doused with perspiration. But Ian didn't know the cause, for it was his first experience with Southern humidity.

Eventually, Ian's hand wave caught the eye of a taxi driver who pulled over at the curbside. "Can I take your suitcase?"

"Yes, please."

"Wheah to?"

"A decent hotel near Bealle Street and the Monarch Saloon, please."

"Okay, I know one."

On the way to the hotel, the driver was engrossed in a song on the radio while Ian gazed out the cab's windows, worried that he might have made a serious mistake. After all, he knew no one and no one knew him or expected him. Anything could happen. While he fretted about all that could go wrong, the cab driver pulled into a moderate hotel parking lot, one block south of the Monarch.

"I think you'll like this place. Monarch jest up ahead," as he pointed ahead with a nod. "That'll be three dollars and eighty-five cents."

"I see. Thank you. Keep the change," Ian said as he handed the driver a five-dollar bill.

Judging by the empty parking lot, Ian assumed the hotel had plenty of vacancies. Upon entering the hotel lobby, Ian first noticed an elderly white man with an unlit cigar in his mouth working the counter.

Ian wondered whether the cigar or a poor disposition caused the man to frown continually. Ian wasn't too concerned with the condition, as long as it was not too drastic and he could feel safe. Ian grabbed a bowl of broth and hot tea at a small café across the street. Afterward, he crossed back to his hotel, observing his surroundings as he walked. The surly attendant was still there, working his cigar from side to side, listening to country music on his AM radio.

"Excuse me, Sir, but I wonder if you could assist me? Do you know what time the blues men start playing at the Monarch tonight?" Ian asked.

"Huh? Oh. Don't know," answered the hotel attendant in a gruff tone.

Ian decided it was his temperament, and not the cigar, which caused him to scowl. He then returned to his room and lay on the bed, mentally rehearsing his itinerary for the night. At half past seven, Ian scurried down the sidewalk to the Monarch. The place was filled, and seeing an empty stool at the bar, Ian grabbed it quickly.

"What'll ya' have?" asked the bartender.

"Nothing, thank you."

"Nuttin'?" replied the bartender in a rather perturbed tone.

"Well, a Coke, please." The soft drink order was merely to appease the obviously upset bartender. Ian didn't really care for alcohol since his dad's two brothers had died from cirrhosis of the liver. He knew, too, that he would need all of his mental faculties while researching the blues men and their surroundings.

A small band of blues musicians played that night. For a brief moment, Ian visualized himself at the unoccupied piano bench. For the next two hours, he sauntered around the Monarch, trying his best to incite discussion of the blues with anyone who was willing. He spoke with several people, and one fact became very evident to Ian. Somehow, he must travel to the Mississippi Delta. That was what Ian kept hearing, that the blues stemmed from there. Two of the bar's patrons told Ian that the blues were discovered by W. C. Handy near a train depot in Tutwiler, Mississippi, near the turn of the twentieth century. Ian was further informed that the Delta was just an hour's drive from Memphis. But how would he get there? Perhaps he could rent a car from someone. But from whom could he rent it?

Ian then encountered an unprecedented stroke of luck. Although it did not seem so at the time, Ian was fortunate to lose his place at the bar when he ambled around, inquiring about the blues. He looked desperately around the dark room and spotted a table occupied by an unkempt man wearing a dirty baseball cap.

"May I sit here?"

"Huh? Oh, I reckon'."

"I am Ian Smythe."

"Ian?" slurred the inebriated man, oblivous to the band or the other surroundings.

"Yes."

"Can't say I evuh huhd that name."

"It's British."

"British? You frum Scotlin'?"

"England. Cambridge, England. How do you like the band?"

The man continued to look down at his drink. "Huh? Oh, I reckon' they all right. That ain't why I'm here."

"No?"

"Naw." The man paused. "I'm here so I kin drink away my sorrows. I'm Eagle. At least, that's what people call me. Real name's Willis Williams."

"Pleased to meet you, Wil—I mean, Eagle. Why are you trying to drink away your sorrows?"

"Might as well. Wife left me fur 'nuther mechanic. Took our two daughters with her. Ain't heard from 'em in three days. Bills are startin' tah pile up. Got a car out in the parkin' lot that I need tah sell."

"Would you by chance like to rent it?"

"Ain't never thought 'bout rentin' no car. How do you do it?"

IAN DROVE south on Highway 61 toward Clarksdale, MS, while Robert Johnson's *Cross Road Blues* blared out of Willis William's AM radio. The last road sign informed Ian that he was eighteen miles from his destination--too far to reach with the little gasoline his gauge indicated. Ian searched for his map on the front seat under all of the papers, clothes, candy, and empty soft drink bottles. After finally locating it, Ian discovered that there were no other towns noted before Clarksdale. A Monarch patron had informed him that there was a small store north of the town, but Ian wasn't told whether or not they sold fuel.

While Ian continued to drive down the two-lane asphalt highway, several things puzzled him. Why do Americans drive on the wrong side of the road? Why do they have the steering wheel on the opposite side of the vehicle? Why do Americans insist on using miles as a measure rather than kilometers? Would he ever get used to the States' monetary system? What did the locals call the white-tufted crop he had been seeing for approximately sixty kilometers? Occasionally, Roger passed a small group of decrepit houses dotting the Delta flatland. He wondered if human beings actually resided in those pitiful shanties.

Ian needed fuel soon. He stopped his car when he spotted a small group of black boys and girls playing in front of one of the homely shacks. One of the boys swung a stick in his hand as several barred Plymouth Rock hens and a malnourished blue tick hound occupied the sparse, wild grass of the front yard. Over to one side sat an old, rusty, 1949 International pickup truck minus its tires and tailgate. In the distant background, Ian spotted a rotted out plywood basketball backboard and netless goal.

"Excuse me, I wonder if you might assist me?" Ian asked the children.

Puzzled with Ian's British brogue and choice of words, two of the black boys—shirtless and barefoot--and one of the girls walked sheepishly out to the road where Ian had stopped.

"I am looking for Happy's Filling Station. I was informed that I would come to it prior to my arriving in Clarksdale. Is my information correct? Can you tell me how much farther?"

Still confused, the wide-eyed trio looked at one another. Slowly, they raised their arms toward the south. The boy holding the stick replied, "Mistuh, you ain't got fah tah go tah Happy's." While pointing southward, he added, "It jest ovuh dat next hill yon-duh."

"Thank you. Oh, by the way, is that stick you are holding your baseball bat?"

"Uh-huh."

"Well, what are you using for a baseball?"

"Dese heah."

"What are *those*?"

"Dese? Dese be sweet gum balls."

"Oh. Well, thank you so kindly. Good day to you, Gents. Oh, and The Miss."

Expressionless, they merely looked at one another as they watched Ian continue down Highway 61.

In a moment, Ian had made his way to Happy's. Pulling up to the sole gasoline pump, Ian observed its age, conspicuous slope, and paneless glass window. Four elderly black men sat on an old church pew in front of the station. Two of the men were playing dominoes while the third blew a lazy tune from a cheap harmonica. Happy, the fourth man and the store's proprietor, stood and avidly watched the game of dominoes. But all playing ceased the moment the stranger pulled into the lot. The foursome, attired in normal fashion for Delta black men of the day, were baffled that a white man would stop at Happy's.

As Ian exited the car, he wiped his neck with a handkerchief. "Good day to you, men. It is dreadfully hot here, isn't it? It must be at least thirty-five degrees. How does one tolerate such heat?"

Happy paused for a moment after swatting at a fly on the nape of his neck. Ian's accent had the men a bit confused. Happy replied, "Well, suuh. We'z kin tell you ain't from dese pahts, else you knowd it's lack dis all summa lone. An' you *sho'* can't be from dese pahts if you thankin' it only be thuhty-fi dah-grees. Must be close tah a hundrud out heah."

All four black men chuckled. The harmonica player added, "An' it ain't fixin' tah let up no time soon, needuh." The other three men nodded in agreement. Ian observed that the harmonica player glared straight ahead, rarely moving his head. A crooked stick lay beside him, propped up against the pew's edge.

"Oh, that's right, you use Fahrenheit, don't you? I am afraid I am still using Centigrade for the temperature." Ian struggled to remove the gasoline pump's nozzle. "Could one of you gents show me how to work this petrol mechanism?"

Happy Jefferson, a black man of about fifty-two with a slight limp in his right leg, trudged over to help Ian. Happy was a respected member of the black community and a deacon in the Mount Nebo Missionary Baptist Church. Many of the local blacks looked to Happy for help during the hardest of times. Frequently, when they did not have ready cash, Happy let them buy on credit.

Few blacks in the Mississippi Delta were proprietors of anything. That's just the way it was. The whites even owned the sharecroppers' homes in which many blacks resided. Most black folks could only dream about becoming owners of land, homes, and automobiles.

"Gotsta' know dah comb'nashun tah dis ol' pump," says Happy, as he quickly and effortlessly placed the nozzle back into the side of the pump. "Ain't wuckt jest right in a lone time. B'sides, I wudn't 'xpectin' you tah pump yo' own gas. It jest take me a minit tah git ovuh heah tah hep you wid it. I's gotsa' bum leg."

"Thank you, Sir. You are very kind. I will take fifty liters of petrol, please."

"Say whut?" asked a bewildered Happy.

"Oh, uh, just fill it up please. Say, perhaps you could tell me. For a little more than sixty kilometers now, I could not help but notice that white stuff on both sides of the road. It is, well, it is everywhere. What is it?"

All four men were taken aback by Ian's question.

"Iz you talkin' 'bout dah cott'n?" asked Happy, toothpick in mouth.

"Cotton? I was wondering what in the devil that is. There used to be many cotton textile mills in my homeland. Unfortunately, they are gradually being closed down due to foreign competition, I'm afraid."

"Say, jest whe-ah is you frum?" asked Happy. "You don't eb'n sounds lack you'z frum Jackson o' Memphis."

"No, I'm not. I'm from Cambridge."

Ian's reply only aroused more curiosity from the four black men.

"Cambridge? Did you say, Cambridge? You boys evah huhd o' it?" asked Happy, as he glanced over at his comrades.

"Not lest it's in Ah-kin-saw," replied Slim Willie, one of the domino players.

"No, it is a city in England," advised Ian.

"Englan'? Y'all heuh dat, boys? He'z frum Englan'!" Happy paused from pumping the gas. "You mean dah Englan' weah *ow-ah* men hept fight in dah Wah?"

Smiling, Ian replied, "Yes, that's it. It's across the Atlantic Ocean. Quite a distance from here."

"By dah way, I'z Happy Jeffuhsun. An' dat deah be Slim Willie, Jeremiah, an' Puhr-cee."

"Hello," said Ian, as he eagerly held out his hand to shake Happy's. "I am Ian. Ian Smythe."

Happy reluctantly held out his hand. White men of the South rarely shook hands with blacks in those days, for racial prejudice had not been removed. Bitter hatred often ran through some white men's hearts. In turn, the blacks often hated the white men. Neither race trusted the other.

"How much for the petrol?"

"Say whut?" Happy asked, in confusion.

"How much do I owe you, Happy?"

"Dat be fi' sixty, if'n you'z talkin' 'bout dah gas. Jest a minit'. I git cho' change," said Happy after Ian handed him a $10 bill.

"Say, perhaps you gents could assist me. I'm here to learn more about music, a specific genre of music, actually. I am anxious to know all I can about blues."

The foursome quickly but conspicuously peeked at one another, quite perplexed.

Slim Willie finally spoke first. "Iz you tellin' us dat you cum all dah way frum Englan' tah luhn 'bout dah blues?"

"Yes, that is correct, Sir. I am enthralled with blues music."

"Man, you gotsta' tah be kiddin' us!" exclaimed Slim Willie. "Ain't nobody, '*specially no white boy,* evah cum heah tah ow-ah co-moon-ty tah luhn mo' 'bout dah blues!"

"Sir, I believe you are Slim Willie? I *have* come here all the way from Cambridge, England, to learn more about your blues music. As I asked around in Memphis, at the Monarch Saloon and other pubs, I was directed to the Delta. I heard one or two gentlemen say I should probably begin my quest around Clarksdale, Mississippi. He also said Indianola, Greenville, and Cleveland were towns I should try to visit. So, I procured a map, and, here I am."

"Well, Suh, if'n you say so," Slim Willie added. "But you'z a fust tah cum *heah* tah studee dah blues. Blues still 'roun', but sum o' dah bands moved off tah Memphis an' Shah-kah-go tah make it big. Can't make much money 'roun' heah playin' dah blues, les'n you play in dah ba-el-houses."

"Did you say, barrelhouses?" Ian asked, rather embarrassed. "I am afraid I am not familiar with that term. What is a barrelhouse?"

All four of the black men bellowed out in laughter. They knew they were conversing with a real greenhorn. "Ba-el-houses be honky-tonks," volunteered Jeremiah. "You know. I reckon' it's kinda' lack dah Monarch you went tah, in Memphis. 'Ceptin' down heah, we don't call 'em pubs o' sah-loons. An' fuh' sho' aint gone' fine no whites visitin' ow-ah ba-el-houses."

"Dat's ra-at," added Slim Willie, "les'n dah white man lookin' fo' one o' his slaves in deah."

"Puhr-cee," Jeremiah continued, "ain't Jim Johnson an' his band still playin' down da' ro-ed at Bobo? An' Henry Bigsby an' his boys; ain't dey still t'gethah playin' dah blues?"

"Yeah, I heah dey iz' sumtimz' stayin' up in Stovall an' Allagatuh', too. Playin' at all dah night clubs on Sat'dy night," replied Percy. "Dat's 'bout dah only time you kin ketch 'em playin'. Mose uthah' times dey wuckin' fo' sum rich white boys at dah mill o' Mistuh' Simpson's fertilizin' plant. Ain't much else us black men kin do 'roun' heah fuh' money. An' eb'n dat ain't much."

"Just a minute, please," requested Ian, as he hurried back to his car to retrieve a pencil and notepad. "Now, let me see, did you say, Bobo?" he asked as he began to record townships the men mentioned. "And where else? Stovall? And what other cities?"

"Cities?" asked Happy, rather curiously as he held onto his galluses with hooked thumbs. "Dey ain't no cities 'roun' heah" 'cept Clauksdale. Yo' gotsta' go all dah' way tah Clevelun o' Lelan' b'fo' yo' cum' tah eny city. Jest little places on dah ro-ed, Bobo an' Stovall is. I reckon' one could prob'ly check Tutwiler an' Vance fo' sum mo' playuhs. Don't go tah dem ba-el-houses myself. I goes tah chuch' on Sundee."

Ian struggled to speak due to his anxiety. "I *must* find this Jim Johnson and his band members!"

"Hol' on jest a minit," said Happy. "You don't 'spect tah go in dem ba-el-houses, do yo'?"

"Why not? I have money."

"No, I didn't mean cuz' dah money. B'sides, I don't thank dey chaj' tah git in, no way. I mean you'z white. Dese ba-el-houses is fo' black folk."

"Do you mean they won't let me in due to my skin color?"

"Man, yo' really is a greenhone', ain't ya'," Slim Willie asked rhetorically. "It ain't cuz' ah dah money. Lack Happy dun sayed, dey don't cha'j tah git in. But dah secon' yo' step yo' white hiney in deah, ev'ry eye'z gone be on you."

"Will my life be in danger?"

"Nawh, not lackly," added Jeremiah. "Dey'z gonna' wondu' whut yo' doin' in deah do'. I kin tell ya' dat."

"Well, I will take my chances. I didn't come this far to be turned back."

"Ah-ite, ah-ite," said Happy. "But I gotsta' know. Whut you gone' try tah do, wrat down deir songs, o' whut?"

"Oh no. I purchased recording equipment while I was in Memphis. I am going to record their songs if possible."

"Re-co-din' 'quipment?" asked Percy. "What's it do?"

"Come here. Let me show you in the trunk of the car."

Percy remained seated, but the other three cautiously followed Ian to his car.

"Is *he* not going to see?" Ian asked as he nodded toward Percy.

"Won't do no good fo' 'eem tah cum ovah heah," Slim Willie answered. "Puhr-cee be blind."

Ian's first instinct was to apologize; but instead, he remained silent and showed the men the latest reel to reel recording equipment and its different components.

"I can actually record your voices."

"Ah-ite, if'n you say so," said Jeremiah, with skepticism.

"Here, I will show you. If one of you gents will assist me in getting it out. A bit heavy, I'm afraid."

Happy helped Ian remove the equipment. They carried it over to the pew, next to Percy. The black men did not know what to make of it. Although Percy could not observe the equipment, his curiosity was just as aroused as the other three men's.

"Do you have a receptacle?"

"A whut?" asked Happy.

"You know," Slim Willie said, "A rah-sep-tah-kel. Whe-ah kin he plug it in?"

"Oh," Happy said, "Rat-che-ah."

Ian assembled the machine in a matter of minutes. "Okay, say something."

All three black men were reluctant to speak at first.

"Dis heah Happy Jeffuhsun."

"Say something else," Ian suggested.

"An' dis heah be Jeremiah, Slim Willie, an' Puhr-cee."

"Okay, that's good enough," Ian said, as he rewound the tape and began to play it back.

"Wull I'll be!" Happy exclaimed as he handed Ian his change from the $10 bill. "Listen, I don't want nuttin' tah hap'n tah ya'. And mose likely, nuttin' will in thim ba-el-houses. Be ca-fel. Blacks don't cott'n' tah stranjuh's too easy. It ain't dat' dey'z impolite. It's jest dah way it is."

Ian packed his recording equipment in the trunk, not knowing how he should respond to Happy's advice. Getting into his car, Ian commented, "It was nice meeting you, Gents. Maybe on my way back to Memphis I can stop again."

Jeremiah and Slim Willie returned to the pew to resume playing dominoes.

"Okay, you do dat'," said Happy.

While he started the car, Ian gazed up at Happy as he stood near the driver's door.

"Good day to you, Happy. And thanks again." Suspecting that Happy still had something on his mind, Ian asked, "Is there something else that you would like to tell me, Happy?"

"I reckon' dey *is* one mo' thang. Dey's quite a few mo' playin' dah blues. Mose lackly, you kin fine sum ah dese boys in one o' dah ba-el-houses, tonight, wid dis bein' Sat'dy. Nobody tolds ya' though—me, Jeremiah, Puhr-cee, o' Slim Willie—dat dey'z one blues player better'n 'em all. Evee-body knows it, too. Better'n Johnson, Henry, o' eny uthah blues man."

Ian held his breath with the anxiety of a little boy opening a new toy from its wrapper. "Really? Who is he?" he asked, grabbing his pencil and paper from the car seat.

"Quincy Qualzs. Ain't no doubt he's dah best blues player in dah' whole Delta. Kin play mose anythang. Got a ra-at good singin' voice, too."

"Where might I find this Quincy? Did you say, Quincy Qualz?"

"Dat's right. I thank sum folks pro-nounces it 'Quarles.' But 'dat's just dah problem. I can't tell ya' where'z tah fine 'eem. Nobody knows whe-ah he'z gone show up. He might shows up at a ba-el-house neah heah tonight, but den again, he might not cum through heah fo' 'nuddah six months. Can't never tell where'z he gone be.

"He'z been playin' dah blues all my life, an' longah. I 'member hearin' 'eem play when I'z jest a chile. Don't know jest how long he'z been playin'. Coulda' made it big in Memphis or Ch'cago if'n he wanted tah. But peoples say he don't ca-eh nuttin' 'bout dat'. I don't really know why, cuz he coulda' made lotsa' money. So, he jest stays 'roun' dese pahts. He's a huhmit, an' nobody know weah'z he stays."

"Where he *stays*?"

"You know, weah he libs. Nobody knows if'n he libs in a share-croppah's house, in dah backs of a ba-el-house, o' jest whe-ah. He's a huh-mit, I tell ya'. Fo' all's I know, he might be libin' in dah woods sumweah neah heah. He jest shows up frum time tah time."

"Great! I will do my best to find this recluse, Quincy Quarles."

Happy gave a slight nod. "My advice tah you is jest fine dah ba-el-houses south o' Clauksdale. Can't never tell; Quincy and his boys might show up. But fo' sho' you kin heah somebody playin' t'night 'roun' Bobo o' Alla-gatuh'."

"Thank you."

Happy watched Ian exit the store lot, wondering what would become of the stranger from England, visiting the barrelhouses of the Mississippi Delta.

Three

4:45 PM, that same Saturday
Bobo, MS

IAN DROVE INTO BOBO while he waited for the barrelhouse to open. He was exhausted from the protracted visit to the Monarch the night before. Sleep would be good now, he thought. Looking for an area to pull over and park, Ian eventually spotted a small, vacant, gravel lot. One ancient, dilapidated building with chipped paint and broken windows stood in the middle of the lot. The entrance's punctured, wooden door was open, reflecting past neglect. Wild grass had begun to sprout through the cracks of the concrete island where gasoline pumps had once stood.

Ian parked in the back to avoid being seen by curious passersby. He nodded off to sleep. Four hours later, he awoke with vigor and anticipation for the night's opportunities. A glance at his watch showed it was nearly nine o' clock. Tired and hot, Ian started the rented car and headed south on Highway 61. Memphis Minnie's *Bumblebee Blues* played on the radio. Ian had traveled approximately one mile before he saw several car headlights approaching. Hoping he had found a barrelhouse, Ian decelerated, pulling into the dimly lit, gravel parking lot where other drivers had stopped. He couldn't help but notice that the patrons in the cars just ahead of him were all black!

By the time Ian parked and exited his car, everyone else had already entered the seedy juke joint. A red Schlitz Beer sign was loosely affixed above the door. The name of the place had faded on the white wall, but Ian thought it read "Bennie's." Upon entering, Ian found it to be exactly as he had been told. *Every* eye *was* fixed on him! Several thoughts raced through his mind as he stood just inside the door. Ian suddenly recalled Jeremiah's foreboding: "Dey's gonna' wunduh whut you doin' in deah. Dey's gonna' wunduh what a white boy lack yo'self be up to." Ian wondered, "How can I prove to everyone, black and white, that I am here merely to help enhance my music?"

In one corner, Ian noticed a Wurlitzer One More Time Jukebox. Sitting atop the indented record player were several lit cigarettes occupying two large ashtrays.

A Sam Chatmon tune played:

I went down to that river, oh, thought I'd jump and drown.
I thought about the woman I was lovin', boys, I turned around.
I went down to that depot, asked the man...

That was all of the song Ian heard before a large, black woman of middle age, donning a bright red dress, stood directly in front of him. "You lost, boy?" she asked, arms akimbo.

"No, I hope not. I came to hear some blues tonight."

Every patron in the honky-tonk had already glued suspicious eyes on Ian.

"Cum on, now, fo' real? Ain't no white boy evah come in heah dat's I kin recall."

A slim black man of about forty strolled over to satisfy his curiosity. "Where'z you frum?" he asked as he loosely held a can of beer in one hand and a well-used pool stick in the other. "Can't sayz dat I rec-a-nize ya'. An' I thought I knows all dah whites 'roun' dese pahts."

"No, I'm not from Mississippi. I am not even from the States. I am from Cambridge, England, and I am here to research some of the blues players of the Delta. That is all."

With skepticism, the man took a sip of beer before responding. Gazing at Ian, the man continued. "Tell ya' whut, why don't you jest go back t'whe-ah you cum from."

"Why'd you say dat tah dah boy, Eddie?" asked the large black woman. "He ain't doin' no harm as fah as I kin tell."

Ian interjected. "Harm? Oh, no! Like I said, I just want to do research on some blues musicians. You see, in England, we don't have anyone so gifted at writing and singing the blues. A few years ago, I heard my first blues song when some of your local blues men visited our country. That inspired me to obtain a few blues albums. But the more I tried, the more difficult it seemed for me to play like them. I wanted my music to sound as closely as possible to Muddy Waters, Big Bill Broonzy, and some of the other talented blues men. But I still was not satisfied; so, I thought I would come to the States to find out more. First, I went to Memphis, Tennessee. There, I was directed to come to the Delta of Mississippi. And here I am."

"No wonduh' you talks so funny," commented the woman. "Heah, I reckon' you kin sit down. Let's sit ovah deah."

"I's Leona, Leona Stokes. Dis heah's Eddie."

"Ian Smythe. I am honored to meet you."

"I ain't nevuh huhd no white boy o' man say tah a black man dat dey's honud tah meet 'eem," replied Eddie.

"Well, *I* am."

"You want sumpin' tah drink?" asked Leona.

"Well, do you have Scotch?" asked Ian, remembering his episode with the Monarch bartender.

"Scotch? Nope, we ain't got dat. Tell ya' what we do have. We have Falstaff an' Old Crow. Dat's it."

"No offense, but I think I'll pass. I would take something to eat, however, if you have anything."

"Ah-ite, I see whut I kin do," replied Leona, smiling.

Ian was beginning to see what the four men from Happy's Filling Station meant. He needed to gain the black men's trust. Then everything would be okay, he thought. But Ian had not gained their trust yet. He even found himself a bit edgy and nervous. It was the first time in his life to be the only white man in any surrounding. And he was far from home!

The other patrons finally decided that Leona and Eddie had the situation under control. Except for an occasional glance, most of the blacks had resumed their own conversations as they watched several men play pool.

"Tell me, Eddie, will there be any blues musicians here tonight? Do you know where Happy's Filling Station is? Happy, the proprietor, and his friends are the ones who told me to come here."

"Oh, so *dat's* how you cum tah Bennie's. Dis' here'z Bennie's Nightclub. Yeah, I knows Happy an' sum o' dem' fella's dat sits out front o' his sto'. As fah' as any blues musicians cummin' heah tahnight, yeah, I s'poz dey be heah in a little bit."

Leona returned with a large plate of barbecue ribs and potato salad. "Heah, try dese."

As Leona set the plate down, Ian looked down with puzzlement. "No offense, but what are these?" he asked shyly.

"Dem's ribs. An' dey good, too. Kilt dat hawg jest yes-tee-dee."

"Yep, dey's best ribs I ever et anywhe-ah," added Eddie.

"Alright," Ian said, as he handed Leona a $20 bill. Ian began to eat his first meal of barbecue ribs. To his great surprise, Ian liked the ribs so well that Eddie and Leona began to chuckle.

"Tole you he'd like 'em," said Leona to Eddie.

"What's the name of the group that will be singing tonight?" asked Ian.

"Group? Don't know dat dey's gotta' name fo' dah band, if'n dat whut's yo' mean," replied Eddie.

"Main man prob'ly gone be Henry Bigsby," added Leona. "He an' his boys play heah mose Sat'dee nights. Dey usually staht 'roun' tin."

"Great! Can't wait!" exclaimed Ian, with great anticipation. In the meantime, Ian made significant progress on his first plate of ribs.

Soon, three black men emerged from the back door. Cigarette smoke clouded the air, making it difficult to see the men clearly. They chatted with a few of the bar's patrons as they walked toward the stage area. In Ian's estimation, the first man seemed to be about thirty years old, and he had a slim build. "He looks just a little older than I," thought Ian to himself. The second man appeared to be fifty years of age. He was carrying a six-string acoustic guitar and stopped near a set of drums that was already on stage.

When Ian could clearly see the last man, he observed that he was also of slim build. He wore a white dress shirt, black polyester slacks, and a brown derby hat. Ian assumed this man to be the legendary Henry Bigsby. Just the way he carried himself made him appear to be the band's leader. Everyone made sure to speak to him as he walked toward the stage.

"Is that Henry?"

"Yeah, dat be him," replied Leona.

The stage did not resemble a stage at all. No elevated platform nor speakers, microphones, nor special lights were present. Like most of Bennie's Nightclub, its wooden floor was deteriorated. The only reason the blacks called that area a stage was because they did not know what else to call it.

"How'z ev'ybody t'night?" asked Henry. "Ev'ybody feel lack boogyin'?"

The nightclub's forty patrons began to respond. "Yeah, do it, Henry, do it James, Chaahlie."

"Ah-ite, let's see whut we kin do, boys."

From that night forward, Ian would come to realize how well the blues could be played with rudimentary, and often homemade, instruments. Ian would come to realize that while more expensive equipment could be helpful, it wasn't necessary. Blues came from experience. It was what the writers had developed from working in the white man's fields. It would always supersede the latest innovative music equipment. Ian chose to not retrieve his equipment from the trunk for this very reason.

While the blues men played, Ian sat anxiously on the edge of his seat. Although Ian realized that this might be his best chance to meet any blues musicians of the Mississippi Delta, he had not forgotten Happy's words: "Quincy Qualz tops 'em all." However, for the time being, Ian was quite content just to hear *any* blues band. It didn't take long for Ian to realize the trio was more talented than those he had heard at the Monarch. Just to be at Bennie's Nightclub was an unforgettable thrill. At that point, little did he know just how the blues and its innovators would change his life.

Shuhley's a' geein' an' a hawin'
I say, Shuhley's a geein' an' a hawin'
I look downs dah row, but I see no un'
Tah dis land o' cott'n, dah white man's friend...

Ian then watched as Henry removed a diatonic harmonica from his shirt pocket. When the bluesman cupped his hands over the instrument, it seemed to disappear. An occasional sparkle from its chrome reflected off the light. He played smoothly and effortlessly. With the palm of his hand, Henry tapped the hackneyed harmonica frequently to remove spittle.

Ian could have listened to the band for the rest of the night. "This is what *I will* learn to do, if at all possible," he doggedly whispered to himself.

Leona motioned with her head for Eddie to watch Ian. "So fah, look lack he tellin' dah truth. He jest wanted tah heah sum blues played. I jest don't understan' it. All dah ways frum Englan'."

For two hours, Henry and his two fellow band members entertained Bennie's customers. Blues players did not take breaks as they did in Ian's homeland. The trio occasionally swigged their beers, and as they set them to the side, they continued to play tune after tune. Cigarette smoke occasionally filled the stage. The men adeptly worked their cigarettes in the corners of their mouths, sporadically inhaling them with squinted eyes.

Ian peered around the room. All the patrons seemed to be having a good time, forgetting everything else. That was what the blues did for a person; it helped one forget his problems for awhile. From pre-dawn to dusk, the typical black man of the Delta was at the disposal of the white man. But, late at night, in the barrelhouses of the Mississippi Delta, they were free from all levee bosses, taskmasters, and plantation owners.

That night Ian was held spellbound, not risking even a restroom break for fear of missing one of Henry's ballads. Finally, the band rose and thanked the crowd. Ian greeted the trio with a standing ovation, causing most of the audience to glance over at him. Black people of the Delta loved the blues, but they were accustomed to hearing it. They may not have been aware that they had been hearing some of the greatest music of all time in their own back yard. However, most of the world did not know it, either. Ian was awestruck with what he had just witnessed. He wanted to call his musician friends in England and let them know how exciting things were. Sadly, however, the luxury of a phone did not exist in the Delta barrelhouses. Ian wanted to speak to the band. As he approached the men, several others were chatting with them. "Mr. Bigsby, my name is---," Ian began.

"I ahready knows," interrupted Henry. "Befo' we got in dah do' good, we dun huhd dat a white boy wuz heah."

Taken aback by his words, Ian changed the subject. "I believe that was the best performance I have ever seen or heard."

"Thank ya'," replied Henry. James and Charlie were listening, for they were just as curious as everyone else by Ian's visit. "We likes to play, me, James an' Chah-lie."

"I have aspirations of playing like that one day," Ian said.

The threesome merely stared at Ian, not knowing how or *if* they should respond.

"Do you know Jim Johnson?"

The men laughed. "Who don't, 'roun' heah," commented Charlie. "He plays mosely lack we do. All ah' us plays 'roun' dese pahts. Bin doin' it mosta' ow-ah lives."

"What about Quincy Quarles; do you know him?" Ian continued.

Henry, Charlie, and James stared at Ian. "Yeah, who don't," Charlie asked rhetorically. "Quincy good. *Real* good."

Ian wanted desperately to continue his interview with Henry and his friends. But Leona sensed it was time to cool it. She did not want anyone to be suspicious, especially with its being Ian's first time there. "Whe-ah you be stayin' tonight?" interrupted Leona.

"I thought I would get a room at the local inn."

"Say whut? Ain't no such thang 'roun' heah."

"Oh, well. I guess I will have to sleep in my car. Do you think Bennie would mind if I parked my car here until morning?"

"Nawh, I reckon' he won't mine. Bennie been dead fo' three yeahs. We jest keeps callin' it 'Bennie' aftah he die 'cause he owned it fo' so lone."

"Who owns it now?"

"Me. Me an' one uthuh woman ovuh at Rud-yuhd be's dah only black women in Co'homa County who owns 'stablishments. Don't cum easy fo' us black folks, '*specially*, black women."

"Oh, fine, great; would you be so kind as to let me park here all night?"

"Yeah, don't sees why not."

Ian remembered Happy's advice to be careful. "Are you quite sure?"

"If I say you kin pahk heah, you kin pahk heah. An' I'll do ya' one bettuh'n dat. I'll be back in dah mo'nin' tah clean up. Bennie installed a shower in dah back ah dah place yeahs 'go. He always havin' tah do sum fix'n up in dah place, so he thought he ma-at as well sleep heah sum, 'spec'ly since he stay so fah 'way. When I cum in dah mo'nin', you welcum tah use dah showuh. I will bring sum towels frum dah house."

Ian was elated at Leona's words. "Thank you so kindly. I can pay you whatever I would have to pay for a room at the inn."

"Nawh, ain't no need. B'sides, you be leavin' t'mah-uh fo' anuthuh co-moon-ty, ra-at?"

"I suppose."

Leona and Ian said good night. Part of Ian wanted to stay another night and hear more of Henry's band. That night, he had heard that Henry and the band often played at Bennie's on Sunday nights, too. But another part of him wanted to move on to another barrelhouse, for he knew his time in the Delta would come to a close soon.

Ian lay in the back seat of his car that hot August night, swatting an occasional mosquito. As he looked up at the stars, he pondered all that had transpired. For three years he had longed to experience something like this. As far as Ian was concerned, it could never get any better than hearing the blues in its birthplace. His goals for the last three years were to write, sing, and play the blues just like these men. He knew of no Englishman with that ability. Ian had made the commitment to learn all that he could while he was there. However, he had not realized the personal sacrifice this would require.

Four

IAN WAS AWAKENED the next morning by a clattering noise. Leona held a half-flattened cooking pan at the back door. She was feeding two stray cats with some of Saturday night's leftovers. Leona saw Ian holding his head up above the window ledge.
"Guh mo'nin'. How'd ya' sleep?"
"Fine, thank you."
"I kin prob'ly cook up sumpin' in heah fo' breakfas', if you want," offered Leona.
"Oh, thank you so kindly."
"Come on in," said Leona, as she led Ian to the kitchen.
"Leona, last night, when I entered your premises, I noticed Eddie wasn't very hospitable to me at first. I'm not sure others were, either. Yet, *you* were. Would you kindly tell me why?"
Leona began suffusing lard in the bottom of her cast-iron skillet as she listened. "Well, all my life growin' up in dah Delta, I bin tempted, even encouraged, tah hate dah whites. Dey wuz seen as slave drivuhs who ca-ed little fo' dah needs o' blacks, who wudn't nuttin' but pieces o' flesh doin' deir duty tah futhuh dah white man's pockit. But when I wuz sixteen, sumpin' happen dat I ain't nevuh fo'got. It cause me tah 'preci-ate sum white men, in spite o' my friends an' fam'ly assuhin' me ut-huhwise.
"One aftuhnoon in town, I wuz wid my mama an' little bruthuh Mahcus comin' outta' Simpson's Gen'l Sto'. Mistah an' Miss James Osbo'ne, a well-respected white couple in dah Bobo co-moon-ah-tee, approached us on dah sidewalk. We knowd who it wuz right off. Ev'ybody know 'em. It be a common teachin' in dah South dat no black male, regahdless o' his age, could stay on dah sidewalk whin a white woman wuz approachin'. N'fac, blacks hab bin lyncht b'fo' jest 'cause dey touched a white woman. But I knows fo' a fac' dat sum o' dem white men bin doin' mo' dan jest touchin' young black guhls. Dat's pahtly why thousand's o' blacks migrated tah Ch'cago between dah two big wahs. Anyway, my little bruthuh didn't know dat rool 'bout gittin' off dah sidewalk whin a white wom'n be comin', but dat wadn't his fault. Mama had nevuh gotten 'roun' tah tell'n' Mahcus 'bout it. So, he din't know. Mistah Osbo'ne pushed Mahcus off o' dah sidewalk whin Mahcus di'nt volunte-ah tah step off. Mistah Osbo'ne say tah Mahcus, 'Niggah, whut you thank you doin' stayin' on dah sidewalk whin a white wom'n be

comin' down it?' My bruthuh an'Mama din't say a wuhd. Blacks nevuh did; dey just accept it as a way o' life.

"At dah time, none o' us seen Wayne Tuhnah sittin' in his pickup truck in front o' Simpson's. At dah time, Wayne wuz a college stoo-dent at Mem-phus State, home fo' dah weeken'. Wayne an' Mistah Osbo'ne knowd each uthuh; in fac', dey's membuhs o' dah same chuch. Wayne seed dah enti-uh in-sah-dint. Gettin' outta' his truck, Wayne stood up tah Mistah Osbo'ne. Mos' people, whites an' blacks, wouldn't da-eh do sech a thang. Wayne say, 'I saw dat, Mistah Osbo'ne. Deah wadn't no call fo' it.' Miss Osbo'ne say, 'Wayne, has you loss yo' mine?' I wuz keepin' my eye on Mistah Osbo'ne, cuz he had his fists clinched, cee-gah in mouth. 'Nawh, Miss Osbo'ne, I ain't loss my mind. But I wuz sittin' in dah truck deah an' saw dah whole thang. Yo' husban' din't have tah push Mahcus.'

"Mama grabbed me an' Mahcus by dah e-ahs an' stahted walkin'. I huhd latuh dat Mistah Osbo'ne ain't fo'got whut Wayne dun tah 'eem in town, showin' 'eem up lack dat. But Mama an' me talks 'bout it latuh. We both 'preciated whut Wayne dun fo' us whin he coulda' jest stayed outta' it. Evuh since din, I don't judge a man o' woman by dey skin, but whut be in dey haht, kinda' lack dah preachah say whin he be preachin'. He say it whut Jesus would do. Dat's why whin you cum in heah lass night, I din't judge you jest cuz you a dif'nt coluh dan me."

"Thank you for relating that to me, Leona," Ian said sympathetically. "It really does help me understand."

Leona and Ian continued to chat as they ate breakfast.

"Well, I must be on my way," Ian said after noting the time.

"So lone," said Leona, smiling.

Leona Stokes had been a regular churchgoer as a child growing up in the nearby community of Rudyard. She quit her junior year in high school to get married. Two divorces and one miscarriage later, she had all but forsaken her church when things didn't go the way she had expected. Leona was determined that she would make something of her life. She received her high school diploma at the age of twenty and subsequently took several correspondence courses from a Jackson business school. Leona jumped at the chance to purchase Bennie's, although she knew that it would create a stigma for life from all of the local black church-going women.

THE BARRELHOUSES WOULD NOT be open for another twelve hours. Ian thought this was the opportune time to investigate the city of Clarksdale, since he had bypassed it after he left Happy's. While *Devil Got My Woman* played on the radio, Ian replayed in his mind the incident with Wayne and Mr. Osborne. He pondered about how his

British comrades would find it hard to believe some of the things he had already seen and heard.

Arriving at the south end of town, Ian noticed that only one or two cars were in sight. It was as if the town had closed up, but Ian wasn't sure why. Halfway around Town Square, Ian noticed a sign for the First Baptist Church of Clarksdale. The parking lot was almost full; likewise, at the First Methodist Church directly across the street. Ian drove beside an elderly man getting out of his car at the Baptist church. "Excuse me, Sir, but is *everyone* in church this morning?"

The gentleman seemed to be surprised at Ian's question. "Surely ah', less'n they ah heathens."

"Well, thank you," replied Ian.

Ian then remembered something that Happy had told him earlier: "I'z go tah chuch on Sun-dee." Ian decided to return to Bobo to see if he could locate Happy's church. Maybe he could learn something about the blues there, he thought to himself. After all, while the elderly white man at the church wasn't exactly rude, he wasn't all that affable, either. Maybe the blacks would be more welcoming. Besides, Ian had come to hear blacks sing and play the blues. And he could already see that there was no chance of finding them and their music in the white churches.

At half past ten, Ian arrived in Bobo. As he drove south on Highway 61, Ian observed that Leona's car was no longer parked at the honky-tonk. He looked for any semblance of a church. Just past Bennie's Nightclub, an aged sign stood at a slant on the roadside. The only legible letters Ian could read were "hur h." Assuming the word was missing its "c's," Ian turned on a small one-lane gravel road that veered to the right. In his rearview mirror, he observed a cloud of dust kicking up behind his car. To the left and right of the road, large tracts of cotton filled the land as far as he could see. After traveling for two miles, Ian came upon an old white building. Its steeple was in desperate need of repair. Ian counted fifteen cars parked around the building. He noted that there were no parking stripes nor signs like the affluent white churches had in Clarksdale. Ian assumed that worshipers parked wherever they could find a spot. A sign stood in the yard: "Mount Nebo M. B. Church." Under this inscription was a phrase that Ian assumed derived from the Bible: "Prepare to meet your Maker."

Ian heard singing inside the moment he exited his car. As he walked up the porch steps, several red wasps swarmed the building's protruding rafters. Ian watched them carefully to avoid becoming their next prey. As he entered, an elderly man in a navy blue wool suit and black crepe shoes began leading the music. Everyone in the choir noticed Ian as he entered; yet, they began to sing—and swerve. To reduce unnecessary attention, Ian quickly took a seat on the back pew.

The choir and the congregation joyfully obeyed each hand gesture of their director.

> Leader: *Put on your warfare shoes,*
> Choir and Congregation: *Rock, Daniel.*
> Leader: *Put on your warfare shoes,*
> Choir and Congregation: *Rock, Daniel.*

Like Leona, Ian was no longer a regular churchgoer. But he had attended enough to know there were significant differences in this church from the Anglican Church of Cambridge, which was very subdued and orderly. His church's paid secretary printed a worship guide from which worshipers never veered. The service was monologue and was easily predictable; all one had to do was read the guide. Furthermore, to add to the monotony, the rector read his sermons. Punctuality was not a factor in the black folks' church; whereas, in Ian's church, everyone seemed to gaze at his watch when the service failed to start and end on time.

Ian quickly discovered that this would not be the case today. This church had no bulletin or church guide. No one was going to tell the blacks of Mount Nebo M. B. Church how to worship the Lord. Spontaneity was a natural component of the service. Even the pastor rarely knew what would occur next in the service. Yet, he did not seem to object, for this was the only place where freedom reigned for a godly black man.

Ian began to notice how his own soul was changing inside. The members' jubilation impressed him deeply. For the first time that he could remember when attending church, he felt *welcome*. Their singing was inspiring, far surpassing anything he had ever experienced. He mused, if it were only like this back in England, he would be the *first* person to arrive on Sunday mornings!

After two more melodious hymns, the leader turned the podium over to the pastor.

"Welcum, ev'ybody," said Pastor Robinson. Pastor Ralph Robinson was a short man, with a protruding paunch and receding hairline. The pants of his black buttondown suit were cuffed. Brother Robinson had been Mount Nebo's faithful pastor for the last seventeen years; but his congregation couldn't afford to pay him. Members were good to supply him and his family with some of their vegetables, an occasional chicken, or goat tripe. Like the majority of his parishioners, Pastor Robinson earned a meager living by working on the nearby plantations as a hand. "I see we have a visitah t'day. Let's welcum 'eem."

Everyone in the congregation turned to eye Ian. A deacon and his wife moved out of their pew to greet Ian while others followed. Unlike his reception at Bennie's, Ian felt warmth from the worshipers. He had never felt so at home in *any* church. "Glad tah have ya'," the couple said. They held out their hands to shake with Ian.

"Thank you, kindly."

After the greeting, the offering was collected. Ian happily put three dollars in the plate, to which the senior usher nodded with a smile. While the offering continued and the musicians played, Ian observed that there were twice as many women present as men, many of whom were trying to stay cool with their funeral fans. After the offering, a large woman from the choir, holding no music sheets in her hand, approached the pulpit. With no introduction, she began to sing.

They took my blessed Lord,
They bound him with a purple cord,
They carried him 'fore Pilate's bar,
They splunged him in the side,
And he never said a mumblin' word,

The choir joined in.

Oh, not a word,
Oh, not a word,
Oh, not a word,...

As Ian listened intently to the soprano dressed in a midnight blue velvet dress with three-quarter sleeves and decorative buttons, he found himself just as mesmerized with her voice as he was when Henry and his band had played. Her apparent sincerity impressed Ian the most.

Next, Pastor Robinson stepped up to the lectern. "Befo' I preach my suh-min, let me say, don't fo'git tah stay fo' lunch. Dah Lawd's bin good tah us." Several "Amen's" were shouted intermittently from the congregation. The lady seated just in front of him whispered mildly three times, "Thank You, Jesus." Never had Ian heard informal dialogue between pastor and congregation.

After the service, an elderly lady sitting directly in front of Ian turned around to speak. "Yo' goin' tah stay fo' lunch, ain't ya'?"

"Well, I hadn't really thought about it, but I suppose I could. Thank you so kindly."

"Ya' welcum'. I'm Sistuh Ruby. Heah, let me intra-duce you tah sum uthahs."

What seemed to Ian an eternity of greeting people was actually a few minutes. But Ian did not complain, for he had never been to a church where so many people were actually glad he was there.

The homemade makeshift wooden picnic tables were in the shaded back yard. The cotton field seemed to envelop the church's property, causing the tables to be placed very closely to one another. Ian did not recognize much of the food before him. Fried chicken, pinto beans, watermelon, cornbread, blackberry pie, and two ice coolers of RC were spread out over two of the tables. Ian recalled how much he liked Leona's ribs. Maybe, Ian thought to himself, someone brought some ribs. Pastor Robinson gave the blessing. Everyone stood in line, taking turns filling their plates. Ian realized some might be offended if he didn't eat what they brought. With a bit of hesitation, he placed a little of everything on his plate. He had never *seen*, much less *tasted*, mustard and collard greens, turkey necks, chitterlings, and fatback. A teenage boy warned Ian to beware of the ant beds scattered around nearby.

Ian sat next to Sister Ruby while the soloist sat across from them. "I must say, you have a wonderful voice," proffered Ian.

"Glad you lackt it. I'm Inez."

"How did you learn to sing like that?"

"Like whut?"

"Like you did. Your voice is as lovely as that of a soprano whom I once heard at the London Theatre."

"Evy'body 'roun' heah sing sum. When we'z all git tah singin,' we gits tah jubilatin' an' shoutin'."

"Yeah, dat's whut we bin callin' it all my life," added Sister Ruby. "Can't say I know jest whe-ah dat word 'shoutin' cum frum. Anyway, we likes tah do it."

"Shouting? Well, I find myself constantly learning more and more about your Southern gospel. In England, I'm afraid there isn't much exuberance—shouting--in the worship service."

"Englan'?" asked Sister Ruby. "You *is* a lone way frum home. Whut brang you heah, anyway?"

"I am attempting to find out all I can about blues music. I am rather fascinated by it. The reason I am here today is because I wanted to hear black folk music. I visited Bennie's last night and heard Henry Bigsby and his band. By the way, isn't Happy Jefferson a deacon he--?"

"Henry Bigsby!" interrupted Sister Ruby. "He play dat devil music. Why, dat ain't nuttin' but ba-el-house, deb-ul music, good fo' dah deb-ul hisself... He be playin' an' dem ill-repute wom'n be dancin' dah Camel Walk, Black Bottom, an' Sweet Tail. Thim floozies be kickt outta' chuch if'n dey tries tah cum in heah!"

Inez hurriedly changed the subject. "Yeah, he is. Happy Jeffuhsen be my cuz'n."

"Oh. Where is he today?" asked Ian.

"Oh, he be heah."

"I am afraid I haven't seen him."

"He sits up front ovuh on dah pianah side," replied Inez. "But aftah' dah offerin's tak'n up, he takes it in dah back wid Eldah Roberts. Dey counts it. Mose o' dah time, he cum back in a few minutes."

"I suppose I was so mesmerized by the jubilating that I missed him."

"Mezma-whut?" asked Sister Ruby, still ruffled by the mentioning of Henry and his band.

"Oh, nothing, really. Very inspiring music."

Happy and his wife finally made their way over to greet Ian. "Well, I knows you wuz heah, but I jest couldn't git ovuh tah see ya' durin' dah suh-vis. Sho' is good tah see ya' 'gin. Dis' heah is my wife, Hettie Lee."

Ian stood up to shake hands with Mrs. Jefferson. While Ian stood, Happy pulled him by the arm out of everyone else's earshot. "Say, did you git tah heah enybody lass night down in Bobo?"

"In fact, I did, at Bennie's. Henry Bigsby, James, and Charlie played for at least three hours. They were remarkable, exuberating, fantas--."

"Okay, good. Don't let dah wom'n folk heahs us talkin' 'bout Bennie's. Dey say all dat's dev'l music. Dat won't go ovah too good heah. I can't let Pastuh Rob'nson know I tolds you 'bout it, neithuh. I'z a deacon heah."

"I'm afraid it's a little too late. I briefly mentioned my going to Bennie's last night and, well, let's just say that Sister Ruby didn't like it."

"No, don't say no' mo' 'bout it at chh-uch."

"Yes, I understand. Since you said most blues bands only play on Saturday and Sunday nights, I thought I would visit Clarksdale tomorrow to see if I can find out anything on Jim Johnson and, of course, Quincy Quarles."

"Dat's what I bin wantin' tah says tah ya'. An ow-ah o' so aftuh you left my sto', guess who cum in?"

"I don't know, who?"

"Quo-tez Quarles."

"Quartez? Did you say, 'Quartez'?"

"Yeah, dat's what I sayed. Quo-tez is Quincy's brother. He cum intah dah sto' yest-i-dee. So, I acksed 'eem 'bout Quincy, whe-ah he wuz dese days."

"Oh, really?" asked Ian, full of eagerness and anticipation. "And?"

"Eb'y once in a while, Quo-tez play dah fiddle wid his bruthuh, Quincy. Eny ways, Quo-tez say Quincy callin' it quits. He say he don't want tah play no mo'. So, it don't make no dif-uh-ence if you fine 'eem now, 'cause he ain't playin' no mo'."

Ian was gravely disappointed, for he certainly had not planned for such devastating news. For the last three years, blues music had consumed his life. In Cambridge, Ian had carefully anticipated basing his forthcoming band on this genre of music. When he returned to England, he planned to cautiously screen and audition potential band members based upon their disposition toward the blues. Their outlook on the blues would carry as much weight as their talent. If a prospective band member held a nonchalant attitude toward the blues, he faced an immediate rejection.

"Well, I appreciate the news." Suddenly, an idea raced through Ian's mind. "Even if I cannot coax Quincy into playing, perhaps I can at least speak to him."

"Dat' bein' dah case, Quo-tez say Quincy stayin' at deir cuz'n's house, ovah neah Stovall. Whin you git deah, look up dey cuz'n, Julius Quolz. "

"Great." Ian wanted to shout for that bit of news, but with one glance at Sister Ruby and her fellow church sisters nearby, he knew to refrain. Happy certainly did not want any commotion, lest his wife get suspicious. "Thank you so much," said Ian. "Hopefully, I can locate Quincy Quarles in Stovall, Mississippi." Ian began to eat hurriedly. Even the people sitting around him noticed it. But Ian felt the sooner he arrived in Stovall, the better. He thanked everyone and then trotted to his car. He bade one last goodbye to Happy Jefferson. Although Ian had only known Happy for a day, he felt he had gained a friend for life.

Ian checked his map and located Stovall. It was three in the afternoon. He estimated he could easily be in Stovall within an hour; but Ian had not anticipated what awaited him a few miles down the road.

Five

THREE MILES OUT OF Bobo, Mississippi, on an isolated stretch of road, Ian looked in his rearview mirror to see a car following with its blue lights flashing. After pulling over, Ian noticed two men seated inside the car. He watched in his side view mirror as a fat man, dressed in uniform and donning chrome-rimmed sunglasses, struggled his way out of the front seat. Ian observed an emblem on the driver's door as it opened. The other man, with greasy black hair, sheepishly exited the passenger's side. As both men approached Ian's car, Ian could see that the left side of the deputy's mouth looked swollen.

"Is there a problem, Officer?"

The deputy paused with hands on hips, spitting some of his tobacco juice onto the pavement. "Problum?"

The other man, middle-aged and dressed in civilian clothes, stood behind the deputy. "That's him. That's thuh nigrah' lovuh I seen gettin' out at thuh Mount Nebo church."

"What of it? Is it illegal?" Ian asked, as he read the officer's badge name: Deputy Sheriff Tom Purvis.

"Boy-ah, you know who you talkin' to?" asked Deputy Purvis with a sardonic tone. Before Deputy Purvis continued, he spat again. "See that ra-at theuh?" he asked as he proudly pointed toward his badge. "I'm thuh dep-ah-tee she'iff o' Co'homer County. Don't git smart with me. You'll fine yo'self in a whole heap o' trouble."

"I wasn't trying to be smart with…"

"Tell ya' what, jest git outta' thuh car, boy-ah!" Ian obeyed, stepping cautiously out of the car.

"Tell us, boy-ah, just what in the Sam Hill do you thank you doin' with tha' cuh-luhd folks 'roun' heah? You ma-at do thangs lack that in Ten-ah-see, but you *ain't* gone go messin' 'roun' with 'em heah."

"I beg your pardon! I'm not from Tennessee. I'm from England."

"Heah that, Bill? That license plate says you frum Ten-ah-see. Now, if'n you be frum Englan', what you doin' in that theah automobile?"

"I'm telling you the truth. I'm here to research the black blues musicians of the Mississippi Delta. I rented the vehicle from a man in Memphis. Have I done anything illegal, Officer Purvis? If not, would you please let me go. I'm headed to Stovall."

"Stovall? Tell you what, boy-ah. We white folks keep tah ourselves heah in Co'homer County. And the black folks, they stay tah theirselves. That's the way ev'body likes it. And we plan tah keep it that way." Deputy Purvis paused to spit again. "Got it?"

Ian merely looked at the two men, waiting rather patiently and silently for permission to leave.

"You a Jew or sumpin', o' maybe one o' them communists?" asked Deputy Purvis.

Ian shook his head.

"If'n I heah 'bout any mo' of yo' befriendin' eny nigrah's, you'll be meetin' me 'gin," Deputy Purvis warned. "Get me?" Deputy Purvis wanted to be sure he got his point across. Pulling out his nightstick, he began flipping it against the side of his leg. That was his way of threatening anyone he deemed a rebel.

Ian remained silent, slightly leaning against the hood of his car.

Deputy Purvis was itching to impress his friend in some way. Quickly ramming his nightstick into Ian's midsection, he yelled, "You didn't answer me, boy!" Ian stooped over and fell onto the ground, grimacing in severe pain. The deputy glanced over his shoulder to see if Bill seemed impressed.

"Don't worry, boy-ah, I ain't gonna' hit ya' 'gin, 'lessen cose, I heah you messin' with tha' cuh-luhd folk 'round he-uh 'gin."

Coahoma County Deputy Purvis and Bill got back into their car and slowly drove off. Ian was still stooped over in pain as he strained to enter his car. Lying in the front seat, Ian soon blacked out.

Four hours later, he awoke and struggled out of the car. As he stooped over and looked down the road to the north, Ian made an oral commitment: "I *will not* let these men prevent me from fulfilling my passion!"

Driving on to Stovall, Ian was listening to John Lee Hooker's *No Shoes* on the radio. Ian thought of the bitter irony he faced, rejected by his own race, yet accepted by another.

Six

DUSK WAS SETTLING when Ian arrived in the slumberous town of Stovall. His stomach was still hurting from the deputy's "lesson." Like most other Delta communities, Stovall was comprised of a few white landowners and the black sharecroppers who worked the land. As usual, there were the local Baptist and Methodist churches. The blacks always had their churches, too. The rich, white landowners usually paid for the black churches to be built. Thus, legally, the whites still owned their buildings and land. Whites felt it was wise to let the blacks worship in their own churches, lest they try to enter the white man's.

Happy Jefferson did not know Julius Quarles or where he lived. Ian would have to find Julius' house himself. He decided that he would stay clear of the white man when possible. So far, he had not met one white man of the Delta who actually welcomed him. However, *every* black man had received him. A few of the blacks had at first been suspicious of Ian. But, thought Ian, they had every reason to be.

Driving north on Highway 1, Ian approached a sharecropper's old house. Even for a foreigner such as Ian, the surroundings had become easily recognizable. The front yard typified the usual sharecropper's, sprinkled with wild, sparse grass. The house's wretched condition epitomized most poor blacks as well: squalid, a porch with deteriorated joists; missing window panes, some replaced with board planks while others merely remained open to the Delta's climate. Off to the side of the house was an old wooden plow leaning against a cedar post. No lights were on in the house, which caused Ian to think that it was probably vacant. Its condition was far worse than the others he had observed.

Walking a few steps from his car, he heard someone yell out from the shack. "Who is it?"

"Hello, my name is Ian! I am looking for Julius Quarles."

There was a long pause. "Don't know 'eem!"

Ian doubted the man's sincerity. He felt that in such a small community all blacks would know each other. "Please, are you certain? I am looking for Quincy, Julius' cousin. Do you *really* not know Julius?"

"Said I don't."

An August thunderstorm was brewing. Occasional streaks of lightning flashed across the western horizon, with sudden claps of thunder.

"All right, then. Thank you." Ian returned to his car and left, having never set eyes on the man inside.

Ian continued north on Highway 1 and came to another sharecropper's house, one which appeared to be in better living condition. After one rap on the door, a small black boy, clad only in underwear, came to the door.

"Yes, is your mother or father here?"

The little boy stood there silently, gazing at the white stranger. In a moment, the boy's mother came to the door. "Yeah, what is it? You lost?" she asked, as if the man were intruding.

"Well, I am not sure just yet. I am looking for someone. Julius Quarles. Would you happen to know him or know where I might find him?"

"Yeah, I know 'eem. He's a sharecroppuh' lack mose o' us 'roun' heah."

"Great! Look, Julius is in no trouble or anything like that. Actually, I am looking for his cousin, Quincy. I was told he is currently staying with his cousin, Julius."

"What yo' want wid *dem*?"

"I have been told Quincy is the finest blues player in the Delta of Mississippi. Then, later I was told he had quit playing. But even if that were true, I wondered if I might talk with him. Please, I mean no one any harm."

Suddenly, Ian crouched over with his hands on his knees.

The woman noticed his agony. "What wrong wid' you?" she asked in a half-hearted tone.

"Oh, I had a little trouble with the sheriff's deputy back a few miles. He told me to leave all the nig—I mean, all the black folks, alone. He said if I tried to befriend any of them, he would teach me a lesson, and the next time it would be worse."

The woman and her son stood there silently as Ian struggled to stand erect again. Seeing that he was getting nowhere, he turned to go back to his car. A drizzle of rain began to fall.

"Wait a minute. I guess you tellin' dah truth. Cum in if'n you want."

"Thank you, kindly," Ian replied with what little smile he could manage.

This was a momentous occasion for Ian. It was the first sharecropper's house he had ever entered. He came from a middle-income family of Cambridge. Until that moment, Ian had not realized just how little a sharecropper owned. Two rooms and a tiny kitchen, with no bathroom or electricity. Just one, small coal oil lamp, and no furniture to speak of.

Sharecroppers rented farmland for a combination of cash and a percentage of their cotton crop. Sharecropping began after the Civil War when penniless, free slaves worked farmers' lands. In return, the sharecroppers would receive seed, animals, and equipment in return for approximately half the profits. While it seemed a decent proposal to the freed slaves, it tended to keep the blacks dependent on little profit due to the white landowners marketing the crops and keeping the books. A sharecropper was then at the mercy of whatever the landowner said. He could, and often did, lend the sharecroppers cash, but at exorbitant rates. Most blacks had little education, thereby decreasing their complaints of usury. They were caught in the system, to live out their entire lives possibly on one plantation.

Several small children sat on the wooden floor. Gaping cracks between the two by eight flooring revealed the dirt below. The children seemed to be deathly afraid of this strange white man. Never had a white man entered their home except to pick up seasonal laborers. Occasionally, the white deputies came through looking for an escaped prisoner from Parchman State Penitentiary. The authorities knew that the prisoners' relatives would often harbor them from the law. But for the most part, each race more or less kept to their own kind.

"I kin tell you a litt'l bit. My name's Josephine. Dese be my chillens'. My man ain't heah ra-at now. Good thing, too, 'cause if he knowd I speakin' tah a white man, he might git all mad."

"My name is Ian. Hello, boys and girls." They remained silent. Ian felt that they had been trained not to speak to whites. An idea popped into Ian's mind; he remembered the candy in the car. "I need to be excused for a moment. I'll be right back." Josephine carefully watched Ian through the porch's sole casement. Returning with a paper bag, Ian gave each child two pieces of hard peppermint.

"Bin a lone time since deah eyes all got dat big," Josephine said. "Dat cuz dey ain't seed no sto'- bought candy in a lone time. What you say?"

"Thank ya'," replied most of the children.

"You are quite welcome."

Josephine became a bit more trusting and willing to talk. "Yeah, you huhd right. Evee'body know Julius. He an' Quo-tez both say Quincy callin' it quits. Fifty plus yeahs o' playin' is all he want. You passed Julius' house back 'bout a mile."

Ian remembered passing only one other sharecropper's house. "Do you mean the one with an old plow over to one side and broken-out windows, back about a mile or so south?" Ian didn't tell Josephine that he had already stopped there.

"Yeah, dat be it. Dat weah Julius stayin'."

"Well then, I shall visit that house. Thank you, kindly, my dear. And good night, Gents and Girls. But before I go, I wonder if I might use your facilities."

"My whut?"

"You know, your facilities. Oh, I'm sorry, I mean your restroom."

"We ain't got no restroom—at least, inside."

"Oh, dear. Who owns this house?"

"White boss man. Mistah Johansson."

"You mean he won't provide you with an inside restroom?"

Josephine stood there silently. She would not say anything against the white man; the potential penalties for doing so would be too severe.

"We'z an outhouse out back. You welcum tah go deah."

"Might I borrow a brolly?" Ian asked out of ignorance.

"Say whut?"

"You know, a parasol, a bumbershoot. Oh, I'm sorry, I mean umbrella. May I borrow your umbrella?"

"We ain't got no 'mbrella. Sah-ee. Bertie, shows 'eem weah dah outhouse be," instructed Josephine to her oldest son. Josephine handed Bertie the lantern. It was dark outside, and a steady rain was falling. When they reached the outhouse, Bertie gave Ian the lantern. While there, inside that tiny structure of a building, Ian realized that he had taken many things for granted.

Soon, he returned to the front porch, where Josephine and the children were waiting. Handing Josephine her lantern, Ian thanked her and the children once again.

AS THE RAIN began to pour heavily, Ian returned to Julius' house. Through his windshield, he could see a dim light in the house. Ian was learning that very few of the sharecroppers had such modern conveniences as electricity and indoor toilets. Just as the first visit, a voice yelled out before Ian could get to the door. Ian ran to get onto the porch to avoid getting wet.

"Who is it?" the voice rang out.

"It is I again, the one who was here about half an hour ago. I was informed that *you* are Julius Quarles. Please, I mean you no harm. I'm on a quest to find Quincy Quarles."

The downpour was making it difficult for Ian to hear any reply. Yet, he felt as if someone were staring at him from inside the house. The top half of the door's screen was missing. After a brief pause, a man who looked to be in his sixties came to the door.

"Yeah?"

"I just want to chat with Quincy or Quartez Quarles. I heard Julius was living here and that he was their cousin. I just want to chat with them about the blues. Also, I would also love to hear them play, but then I heard Quincy had finally quit playing and singing."

The man stood there, silent.

"Sir, I am from Cambridge, England." Ian felt the need to explain more fully. "I had sort of a confrontation with your county law enforcer back a few mi--."

"Hmmph, ain't *my* law en-fo-suh," interrupted the man.

"Oh, I see. Well, he said I am not to fraternize with black folk. But I will eventually have to return to England, possibly never to return. So, I thought I would take advantage of every opportunity I had to meet up with some bluesmen of the Delta.

"I understand that some of these men have made it big and moved off to Memphis or Chicago. But I have been told by Happy Jefferson and others that Quincy tops all blues men. But since he doesn't care for the lights and big times of city life, he has stayed in the Delta while some of his contemporaries have gone on to stardom. Even if he has retired from playing the blues, I would still like to meet with him if at *all* possible."

"Uh-huh. Well, you huhd ra-at. I be Julius Quarles. I bet Josephine down dah ro-ed tole you who I wuz, huh?"

"Well,…"

"Dat's ah-ite. She a pritty good wom'n. Her ol' man's pritty mean tah huh. She prob'ly tole you who I wuz tah git you outta' huh place befo' huh ol' man show up."

"That is correct. But again, I don't mean anyone harm. Do you think that there is *any* way I can speak with your cousin Quincy?"

Julius swatted a mosquito in front of his face. "Quincy's laid it up. Say he'll nevah' play 'gin. Ain't dat he can't still play. His body still up tah playin'. Fo' sho', he kin still play."

"Oh, I see."

Julius continued as he flicked his cigarette out the door to be extinguished by the rain. "Quincy, Quo-tez, an' sumtimz, *I* played wid 'em. We played fo' white folks' pahties, weddin's an' sech as dat, maybe a fish fry o' country dance. White folks paid pritty good money, too. But Quincy had a fallin' out wid' one o' dah rich white man's sons. Wuhd got 'roun' dat Quincy beat dah son wid' a stick. Can't blame 'eem do'. Dat boy had it comin' fo' lone time. I fig-yud dey'd hang ol' Quincy fo' dat. I know dah boy's daddy had sum o' his white boys beat Quincy fo' it. Thangs din cooled off o' bit aftah' dat. Ain't bin dah same since."

"Listen, do you think I could meet Quincy?"

"Can't say fo' sho'. Quincy a good man. Quo-tez, too. Quincy was knowd tah hit dah bottle back in his youngah days. His ol' lady straighten 'eem out on dat. But you gotsta' undahstan', black folks bin slaves 'roun' dese pahts fo' o'ah hunded yeahs." Julius paused for a moment, then continued. "I s'pose I kin tell yo' weah Quincy is. You kin tell him I talked tah you, an' I said it'd be ah-ite."

"Really? Great!"

"Ra-at now-ah, Quincy stayin' in Rosedale."

"Rosedale? I'm afraid I haven't heard of Rosedale."

"It in Bahl-i-vah County. He stayin' close tah dah riv-ah."

"What river?"

"Dah Mis-sip-pee. What'd you thank, what rivuh? Take Highway 1 till you come tah Rosedale. It 'bout thuhtee mile frum heah. Take dah secon' duht road tah da' right once you pass Clovis' Bait Shop in Rosedale. Den, go west 'til yo' can't go no mo'. You'll cum tah a levee. Tuhn tah dah ra-at. Dah ro-ed 'el en' pritty soon, do'. Dat's whin you gonna' have tah walk, 'bout a quota' a mile o' so."

"Heah," said Julius, handing Ian a flashlight. "You fo' sho' gone nee' dis. One uthah thang, got a twelve gauge, double ba-el. Gotsa' a coon hound, too. He probl'y gonna' staht bahkin' whin you git close. Be ca-ful, dat's all I gotsta' say."

Ian thanked Julius and drove off in his car.

THE RAIN HAD STOPPED and the clouds had cleared. The full moon and the stars were beginning to shine down on Highway 1. Fred McDowell's *Careless Love* was playing on the radio.

An hour's drive with Julius' accurate directions had put Ian right where he needed to go. He slowly got out of his car, somewhat afraid in the dark of night. Ian had only walked fifty feet when thoughts of turning back raced into his mind. He had only just met these people of the Delta. Questions, doubt began to infiltrate Ian's thinking. He thought about all that had transpired, and he decided that perhaps it had been a plot by the blacks to get even with a white man. Perhaps sensing that the blacks may have found their scapegoat, he began to feel that he was the man whom they could execute their harbored vengeance upon. Then, Ian had a change of heart. "Too late now. I have to go back to Cambridge one day, and I do not want to have regrets later. I must continue."

After Ian walked the beaten dirt path for approximately one thousand feet, he saw a dim light ahead. A faint sound echoed through the patch of woods. Ian believed the music and light were coming from the same area. Though still fearful and anxious of what may lie ahead, Ian began to jog at a steady gait. The root of a giant white oak caused him to suddenly trip and fall. His flashlight quit working due to the fall; but three light taps on the side of his leg had it working again. Ian held the flashlight low and out of sight. As he edged more closely to the house, the music was now unmistakable. It was the sound of a harmonica. Ian turned off the flashlight, still wondering why Quincy's dog wasn't barking.

Ian listened for more distinct sounds coming from the house. It seemed he heard someone playing the harmonica outside, perhaps on the house's porch. Ian was thankful for the full moon shining down on the narrow dirt path. He stopped occasionally to be certain that he was still hearing the music, while he kept his eye on the light coming from the house. Ian soon found himself surrounded by massive short-leaf pines, swamp oaks and eastern cottonwoods. Bald cypresses also stood nearby due to the scattered sloughs caused by the Mississippi's overflow. The river levee made a twisting turn near the house, enabling the patch of woods to be spared from the loggers' blades.

Ian slithered within two hundred feet of the light. Detecting the outline of a small house, he paced another one hundred feet. He carefully felt his way with his feet to avoid any more tree roots. Ian still did not understand why Quincy's coon dog was silent. Ian then remembered the gun that Julius said Quincy owned.

Ian decided it was best to wait until morning. There was no need to rush when part of the reason he had come was to hear the music. Ian was listening to one of the greatest blues musicians ever. Sitting down at the base of a pine, Ian's only regret was that he did not have his recording machine. Tired from the day's events, he could think of no better way to relax than to listen to the sweet music emanating from the porch.

DAWN BROKE. Ian was awakened by a rough, coarse feeling on his cheek. He quickly recalled how it reminded him of a puppy he owned as a lad. Opening his eyes, Ian saw the Red Bone, tail wagging, emitting an occasional whine.

As Ian sat up, he found himself looking down the twin barrels of a shotgun. A black man in his sixties held a gun pointed at Ian. His sleeves from his white cotton shirt were rolled up on his forearms. A cigarette dangled from the tip of his lips. He was about five feet, seven inches tall with a slim, muscular build. He wore a pencil-thin mustache and a scraggly beard. The man said nothing; he just glared at Ian.

"Hello. You caught me off guard. Please. You don't have to point your gun at me."

The man still said nothing, continuing to point the gun in Ian's direction. The hound tried to put his front paws on Ian. "Down, Slick! Gid-down!"

"Thank you."

"You lost, boy-ah?"

"I don't think so. I am looking for Quincy Quarles. Might he be you?"

The man continued to stare at Ian in silence.

After a brief pause, Ian repeated, "Please, you won't need that gun. My name is Ian Smythe, and I am from England. I am here because I want to learn as much as I can about blues music."

Still staring at Ian with an intense glare, the man spoke again. "Blues, huh? How'd you fine me?"

"Please, are you Quincy Quarles? Because if you aren't, I am wasting your time and mine. I was directed here by Julius Quarles."

"Julius, huh?" After another long pause, the man replied, "Shoulda' knowed I couldn't hide out fo'evah. Yeah, I'm Quincy. But, whut you want wid me?"

"I just want to know more about you, your music. As I was saying, I am from England. A few years ago, some of your contemporaries visited England upon invitation. I was fortunate to hear them play. Being a musician myself—principally, a pianist--I was deeply inspired. However, when I heard these men play, I was also depressed—depressed, because I didn't know how to play as well as they. I wanted to play like them.

"You see, although Britain has many talented musicians, we cannot seem to duplicate your blues singing or playing. So, I thought I would come to America to find out all that I could. I first went to Memphis, Tennessee. Then, I was told to visit the Delta of Mississippi. I found Happy's Filling Station, and I even ate lunch at his Mount Nebo Missionary Baptist Church. Later, I spoke with a Josephine. And then *finally*, I met up with your cousin, Julius Quarles, who told me how to get here."

"You came a lone' way fo' nuttin'. I don't play no mo'," said Quincy, as he thumped his cigarette on the ground. Quincy turned to go back to his house.

Ian pursued. "Please, I didn't plan to come this far only to be turned away."

"You planned wrong, boy-ah. Dun tole ya', I don't play no mo'."

The two men were near the porch. "You might as well go home. I'm sah-ee, but I jest can't do it no mo'."

"You *can't* or you *won't*?"

"I *won't*. Dat's why you wastin' my time an' yo-uh's."

"Please, if you would just let me sit and chat with you for an hour or so, I'll be on my way."

Quincy sat down on a step of the porch. "What is it you wants tah know?"

"Alright, thank you. Tell me, lest I forget to ask later, where can I find your songs?"

"Fine my songs?" If'n you mean on pa-puh, ain't no black man 'roun' heah writ down no wuhds tah his songs."

"I am afraid I don't understand."

"Sonny boy-ah, dey be three reasons why you ain't gonna' fine my blues writ down. Fo' one, mosta' us black folks ain't got no papuh, so whut we gone' writes it on? Secon' reason is, mose' time we don't sing dah song dah same way. Jest 'bout ev'ry time we sing an' play, we change it up lit'l bit."

"Oh, I see."

After a slight pause, Ian continued. "And the third reason?"

"Can't read no' write."

"I am afraid I never thought of that."

"You'z in a diff'nt wuhld. Don't know whut it's lack weah you cum frum, but *dis* is dah *Delta*. Dah white man's dah boss man. Bin dat' way all ow-ah lives. An' it ain't fixin' tah change. I kin tell ya' dat."

Ian was trying to work up enough courage to ask Quincy to play a tune on his harmonica.

"Mr. Quarles?"

"Yeah," he answered, as he drew the last puff of the Lucky Strike before thumping it in the yard.

"Before my hour is gone, would you, uh, would you play your harmonica?"

"I dun tole you, boy-ah, I don't play no mo'. Don't ev'n want tah."

"But I heard you playing last night."

"Last night?"

"Yes, I arrived here last night. Last night, I walked up, right out there. You were playing your harmonica. I just lay there. I don't know how long I listened before I fell asleep. I didn't wake up until this morning when your dog licked my face."

"Hmmh, usetah' be culdn't nobody sneak up on me lack dat. Gittin' old. Can't heah so good no mo'. Lucky fo' you dat Slick wuz out in dem woods lookin' fo' 'possum o' sumpin', 'cause he sho' woulda' let me know you wuz out deah."

Ian was still waiting for Quincy's reply about playing music again. And Quincy was trying to decide if he would play after he had already declined the offer.

Seven

QUINCY ABRUPTLY STEPPED into his house only to return a moment later with a six-stringed guitar in hand. "I don't lacks playin' dah hah-mon-ee-cah till latuh in dah day. Bin smokin' too lone, I reckon'. Fust thing in dah monin', my lungs don't do too good." Quincy slowly placed his guitar strap around his neck and shoulders. Ian observed several hairline cracks in the guitar's belly. He sat transfixed as Quincy played and sang. Although Quincy's voice was somewhat raspy, his slender fingers slid effortlessly up and down the frazzled guitar's neck and bridge.

Dah crack o' dawn,
It cum early fo' dah man,
Dah hinny an' jenny,
I says dah man
Dat wucks wid dah mule.
From can't see to can't see...

Quincy suddenly stopped playing and singing. "I usetah make my own jittahbugs."
"Jittahbugs?"
"Yep, sho' did. Made 'em outta' ol' broom han'ls, wid a coup'l o' snuff bottles an' wi-ah. Sum peoples call 'em one-strang git-tahs. Also callt dah diddley bow. Ain't dat sumpin'? You huhd o' Bo Diddley, ain't yah? Gits his name frum dah diddley bow. I thank his real name be Otha Bates. Mighty fine git-tah playuh, I kin tell ya' dat."
"I would love to see you make one of those."
Quincy continued to reminisce, not acknowledging Ian's comment. "You know, cum tah thank 'bout it, I recall few ye-ahs ago, sum o' dah boys 'roun' he-ah in dah Delta—McKinley, Big Bill Broonzy, Johnson, Chesta', sum' o' dem—goin' tah a fah' country."
"McKinley? Chester? Chester who? I'm afraid I don't know that name, either." Ian frantically tried to memorize the names because he had left his notepad and pen in the car; and he already knew that Quincy would have neither pad nor pen available.
"McKinley be Muddy Watuhs' real name, McKinley Mo'gan. But I nevah huhd no mo' 'bout it whin dey cum back o' nuttin'. An' Chesta' Buh-nett, he be Howlin' Wolf. Don't know if'n Son House, Fred McDowell, Riley—I mean, B. B.--eny o' dem evah left fo' dat country."

"England. I don't know if they ever visited England, either. May I?" asked Ian, as he gingerly removed his harmonica from his pants pocket.

"Sho' thang. I'd lack tah heah yo' style, tah see whut you kin do."

Ian had much more confidence playing the keyboard. But he had tinkered with the harmonica for quite some time, and with a little encouragement from Quincy, he decided to try his mouth organ while Quincy played guitar. Ian had planned to do whatever it took to prod Quincy into playing. Unfamiliar with Ian's harmonica tune, Quincy only had to hear it once all the way through before he began to play rhythm. As the two men played, Ian felt more privileged to be mentored by a poor black, cotton-chopping muleskinner than to enjoy the professional tutelage of his Cambridge piano instructor.

"Yo' know dis' 'un?" asked Quincy, as he began to play one of his favorite tunes.

"No, but I will try to stay with you."

After a few minutes, Ian groaned, "Why can't I play like you?"

"You doin' ah-ite."

"Thanks. Like I told you before, I prefer the piano. I'm a mere tyro at this."

"I lacks dah pianah, too. E'by once in a while, we hab a pianah playah wid us whin we plays in a juke joint."

"I believe something's missing," said Ian in disgust. "Can you tell me what it is?"

Quincy paused. "Well, it ain't dah de-zi-ah. You gots dat. I *thank* I knows whut it is, but ain't fo' sho'."

"What is it?"

"You pritty good wid' dat thang, but deah's one thang I can't teach you. Fact is, don't know dat it *kin* be teacht."

"Oh? What is it?"

"Well, it's lack all us black folks bin knowin' fo' a lone time. Fact is, it take a man dat *have* dah blues tah *sang* dah blues."

For a few brief seconds, Ian's mind returned to the automobile trip he made along his father, when they escorted the visiting blues players to their concert. He remembered one of the blues players in the car saying, practically verbatim, what Quincy had just said: "It take a man dat *have* dah blues tah *sang* dah blues." Ian rose from the old, wooden orange crate used for a chair and stared out into the woods while Quincy resumed playing. Ever since Ian had first heard the blues played by the black musicians in his homeland, he had his heart set on how to play them, too.

But while having the privilege of sitting in front of one of the finest blues players of all time was an unprecedented thrill to Ian, in one way it was disheartening. Ian knew that he would never be as good at playing as Quincy. Quincy had assured Ian that his harmonica playing was better than mediocre, but that didn't satisfy Ian. It wasn't that Ian minded being second to Quincy or any other blues player, as long as he had reached his full potential. He wanted to be sure that he had done all he could when he returned to England. There, he would start his own blues band. But Ian believed that he still had a long way to go.

"Lacks I says, don't know dat it kin be teacht. You cum frum a dif'nt place. Thangs ma-at not be as hard deah. Dis heah is hahd times. And fo' 'nuthah thang, you ain't black."

"You mean, I have to be black to play the blues well?"

"Nawh, I don't thank. But, how's you gone play dah blues when you ain't nevah had dah blues?"

"I'm afraid I don't fully understand."

"It lack dis. You an' me can't tell no woman whut it be lack tah have no baby, now kin we?"

"Well, no."

"An' you an' me, we can't tell sumbody dat we knowd how dey feel whin we ain't bin weah dey bin, can we?"

"I see what you are saying. Therefore, is it impossible for me to play the blues as well as you and the other black men because I haven't experienced the hard times like you?"

"I'd say it is. No mattah' how good you git—an' you pritty good ahready-- until you bin whe-ah we'z bin, you can't sang 'em, 'cause you ain't speer-i-unced 'em. You ain't nevuh chopt cott'n frum sunup tah sundown, plowed wid dah mule in dah heat o' dah day, wuckt fo' a levee camp boss who jest as soon whip you wid his pistol dan tah look at ya', o' bin tole ya' can't git watuh at dah same wah-tuh-in' hole as dah white folk. Dat jest a small paht o' whut I could tell ya', a *real* small paht."

There was a long pause from Ian. "Then, I guess I am going to have to ask you something else; can you teach me the hard times?"

Quincy stood up, with his hands on his hips. "Boy-ah, you really *is* crazy! You don't know *whut* you be sayin'. I can't teach ya' dah hahd times."

For the next fifteen minutes, Quincy tried all he knew to discourage Ian. For starters, Quincy reasoned his age was a detriment. Showing Ian his scars on his furrowed hands and fingers had no swaying effect on him, either. Quincy's cautioning of working in the fields, chopping and picking cotton, hoeing, plowing with a mule, muleskinning, gardening, cleaning varmints, and most of all the physical and verbal abuse by the white man, still did not change Ian's mind. Quincy could see that Ian was one resolute soul, and that his reasons for not teaching Ian were unconvincing.

Quincy related to Ian other setbacks as well. Quincy had seen grown men chop off a hand so that they could get out of working the fields. He had seen some black field hands come up missing for no apparent reason. Usually, it was after they had had words with the white boss man.

"Well, if I paid you, could you teach me some of the hard times?"

"Boy-ah, you *still* don't know whut you be sayin'."

"I think I do. That's how badly I want it."

"I nevah huhd tell anythang lack dis befo'."

"Please," begged Ian, "You would be my mentor."

"Yo' whut?"

"My mentor. A mentor is a teacher, an adviser. That's what I am asking you to become."

"Duz you eb'n know why we calls it dah blues? Fact is, I'll tell ya' whut blues really is. Sumtimes we calls it fiel' hollerin' 'cause we be in dah fiel'd frum befo' sunup tah dahk. Jest tah make dah day pass by, we staht sangin' in dah fiel's, hollerin'. Sumtimes we calls it ol' cone songs. Blues is a kindah vengeance song, I reckon' you could say. It's whut we black labo-ahs felt lack sayin' tah dah white boss, but didn't, lest we wanted punishmen' fo' it. We jest keeps ow-ah mouths shut mose o' dah time."

Ian stood there staring at Quincy, bent on getting his way. "Will you teach me?" he pleaded.

"Whut make you thank I *need* tah do dis? I don't have tah do dis. 'Sides, if'n dah law fine' out you down heah, 'so-shee-atin' wid black folk, dey mat not lack it."

"Yes, I have already met one law enforcer."

"Did? Wheah 'bouts?"

Ian explained in detail the occurrences of his confrontation with Bill and Deputy Sheriff Tom Purvis. Quincy informed Ian that Tom wanted to be the high sheriff, the term blacks had for the top law enforcer in the county, and that it would not have made much difference if Ian had been in another county. Similar results would have taken place.

Undeterred, Ian asked again, "Quincy Quarles, *will* you be my mentor?"

"I'z kin see ya' don't give up dat easy. Listun', it don't make me no dif'ence if'n you becums a bettah' blues playah dan me. I ain't jealous. I ahready knows 'bout all dem blues players dat went no'th, intah big cities. Me, I don't care fo' none o' dat."

"Yeah, I heard."

"You huhd whut?"

"I had heard you were a hermit, a recluse." Ian looked around at the surroundings. "And from the looks of it, I agree."

"Oh, you mean libbin' out heah in dah woods? Hmmh, I guess you could say I'z a huhmit. Fact is…" said Quincy, with a nervous pause.

"Yes? Go on."

Quincy paused and noticed that Ian occasionally scratched his left forearm.

"Fact is, I *don't* like crowds. Biggess crowd I evah bin' 'roun' was in ba-el-house ovah at Greenwood one night. Whin we be wuckin' dah fiel's, choppin' cott'n an' sech, deah be's lots o' us, but we spread out. Fact is, I'm skeered of 'em."

"Why are you frightened of crowds?"

"We, dat is, us blacks, we supah-stishus. My grandmama used tah say, 'If you evah get caught up in a crowd, you gone see ghosts dat night'."

"Really? Just because you were in a crowd?"

"Yep. She say it don't bothah white folks dat libs in big cities. Jest bothah us black folks. Can't 'splain it. But I don't wants tah luhn 'bout it fusthand, needa'. So, I don't go tah no crowds 'cause I ain't fixin' tah be seein' no ghosts. Huhd dat dey 'el buhn you up, make you *real* hot."

Ian resumed his initial request. "Tell me, is it possible for you to teach me some of your experiences before I return to England?"

Quincy lit up another Lucky Strike, thumping his match at a green June beetle scurrying on the ground nearby. "Tell ya' whut, if you el gib me yo' wuhd dat whin you goes back tah Englan', you don't tell nobody how you learnt dah blues, I sees if I kin hep you luhn tah play bettah. But you gone hab tah do as I say twenty fo' ow-ahs a day. No mattah whut I say, do it 'cuz I be teachin' yah frum 'speer-ee-unce. But knows it ra-at now, dat you gittin' yo'sef intah a heap o' huht, and don't go sayin' I din't tole yah, cuz I did."

"We have a deal! I won't tell anyone! When do we start?" asked Ian, with great anticipation, scratching his left forearm.

"Reckon' we kin staht ra-at now. Stay heah, be ra-at back." Quincy soon returned from inside the house, holding a pair of dirty, smelly overalls. Quincy threw them down to Ian, who was standing just off of the porch.

"Heah, put dese on."

"Huh? Oh, no, you don't understand. I have several pairs of jeans and poly-cotton blend shirts in my car. Those won't be necessary."

Quincy took the overalls back and set them down on the porch chair. "Take ca-ah."

"Huh?"

You'z dun tole me dat you wull do enythang I say as long as it make you a bettuh blues play-ah, ra-at?"

"Yes, but..."

Quincy merely stared at Ian.

Ian quickly got the message. "Yes, you are right."

"Fust, you gotsta' taaghtin' up on dem galluses. You git usetah 'em. By dah way, kin ya' cook?"

"No, not really. I always left that to my mother, I'm afraid."

"Well, you gotsta' know sumpin' 'bout cookin' an' eatin' lack we do."

"Oh, what are we having, ribs?" asked Ian, pretending to know something about black cooking.

"Ribs? Nawh. Not tee-day."

"Greens, then? Or chicken?"

"Hmmph, you see. We fixin' tah go tah dah swamp." Quincy walked to the far corner of his porch where he had laid his gun. He grabbed the other four shells from the top of an old cask next to the gun. "I gots two shells in dah ba-uhls and dese fo', so we can't affode tah miss much."

"Swamp? Why? What are we going to do there?"

"We's goin' huntin' fust. Befo' you kin luhn tah cook, you gotsta' hab viddles *tah* cook. Dat's why we goin' tah dah swamp. You know--rabbit, 'pos'm, deer, squel, coon. Maybe a polecat."

The two men departed from the house. Quincy handed Ian a used cloth flour sack that he had sometimes used to pick cotton. "Cum on', Slick."

They walked in the opposite direction of Ian's car; occasionally, the trail paralleled the meandering Mississippi River levee. "By the way, Quincy, why don't you want me to tell anyone in England where I learned to play the blues, assuming I *do* learn?"

"Cuz, I don't want tah have tah luhn mo' peoples. And if dah blues ah' big in Englan' ra-at now lack you say, den dat means dey's gone be mo' peoples wantin' tah cum heah aftah you git back. An' I don't want mo' peoples cummin' heah, 'cuz lack I say befo', I don't lack crowds. Dey gone make me see ghosts if'n dey cum. Dat's paht o' reazun I din't evuh try tah move tah Shee-cah-go o' Saint Lou-eeh. Jest be mo' crowds. An' I dun tole you whut cum wida' crowds."

"Ghosts?"

"Dat's ra-at." While ghosts seemed utter nonsense to Ian, Quincy was dead serious. Quincy often smiled when he spoke, but not when ghosts were mentioned. "You know, I usually don't hunt fo' coons 'cept at night, but seein's how day ain't mech else tah eat at dah house, an' seeins how we can't be picky, I figyaad we'd hunt fo' jest anythang dat we could fine. Ol' Slick gittin' ol, his smellah' ain't as good as it usetah be."

Within a few minutes, Slick had treed a possum in a scrubby blackjack oak. "You evah bin 'roun' a gun whin it be shot?"

Boom!

Ian belatedly held his ears as the possum fell from the tree.

"Ouch!" exclaimed Ian.

"I s'pose you gone git usetah it frum now on," Quincy said with a jocular grin. Slick retrieved the opossum for Quincy, which he methodically placed in the sack. "Thank ya', Slick," smiled Quincy, as he quickly patted him on the top of the head. "Still gots five sha-els, but I'm gone save 'em. 'Sides, dis possum fill us up. Let's go back tah dah house." Quincy handed the sack back to Ian, but Ian held it out at arm's length. On the return to the house Quincy added, "Dat's what 'possum' do. Dey get treed an' mose time dey jest sit deah an' play dead. Dey kin eb'n hang frum deir tails up deah. Dey easy tah-gits, do'. Real easy."

When Quincy and Ian arrived at the house, Quincy suggested, "Jest a minit'. I gets a knife." Quincy returned from the house holding a wooden-handled knife with a ten-inch blade. "Dis 'ell wuck."

"For what?" asked Ian rather naively.

"You see." Quincy placed the possum on an old pine stump that he used to clean critters and fish. As Quincy cut the hide around the neck, Ian began to feel a bit nauseated. "Fust, you gotsta' gut 'eem, git all dem innards out. But dey ain't wasted. Slick!" called Quincy, as he flung the 'possum's intestines to his pet and friend. "Dog gotta' eat, too." Quincy glanced up at Ian. "What wrong widchu? Sumpin' else. Whin I cut dah skin, I be ca-ful as tah not rip it. Dis skin gone be a seat."

"A seat?"

"Yep, you see latuh'." Quincy set the possum skin over to the side.

"Is it necessary to do all of this?"

"Hmmph. Yep."

After several more designed slits of the knife, the opossum was ready for cooking. Quincy wished he had some greens to go with the furry marsupial. He cooked a few potatoes that were temporarily stored on the porch. Then he placed two pieces of hickory firewood in his rudimentary cook stove and waited for the fire to get really hot. Quincy was then ready to boil the opossum in his pan. He let the vermin stew until the meat began to leave the bone, and lastly, he rolled it in pepper meal. "Aw-rat, I thank he be ready."

But Ian was *not* ready. He had never loitered around his mom's kitchen when she prepared meals. After watching Quincy cook the opossum, Ian wondered if his mother had ever resorted to cooking such vermin. He then quickly cast that repulsive idea aside. Even the thought of such made him sick.

"Look, he still be pritty good size aftah he cooked."

Quincy began to eat, while placing a portion of the cooked opossum on a shallow pan for Ian. "What wrong now? Dat pan be clean e'nuff."

"Do you have to ask?"

"Whut'd you thank we black folks duz out heah, in dah Delta? Et bah-bah-kue ribs all dah time? Don't wuhwee, we might git sum ribs befo' lone."

After a few minutes of watching Quincy eat without regurgitating, Ian felt a bit calmer. "Well, I *am* awfully hungry. You think it's safe, you know, for an Englishman to eat that animal?"

"Why not? Ain't nevuh huht me. Whut you thank dah good Lawd put dese 'pos'ms heah fo'? Dey sho' ain't jest fo' lookin' at. I kin tell ya' dat."

Ian finally got the nerve to put a piece of it to his lips. He squirmed and squinted as he bit into the meat while Quincy watched inconspicuously in the corner of his eye. Twenty minutes elapsed before Quincy commented, "Well, look like you finished yo' paht. Want sumpin' tah drank?" Ian nodded with a rather proud look. Eating the opossum was the most difficult chore Ian had ever had to accomplish. Quincy went to the back of the house. "Heah," as he handed Ian an old Mason jar.

"Thank you, I can't say I've ever been this thirsty. Where did you get the water?"

"Down at dah crick. Ain't nevah had no runnin' watuh at dis house. Too fah frum dah ro-ed fo' co-moon-ty watuh an' can't affode tah have no well dug." It was one o' clock before they had finished eating. "Well, let's go see 'bout dat possum skin." Ian watched Quincy adroitly scrape all of the excess meat on the skin's inside with his knife. Ian observed Quincy carefully while he ambidextrously nailed the skin to a pine. Stretching the skin ever so tautly, Quincy advised, "I lets it stay up heah fo' a couple o' weeks tah dry out in dah sun. Usetah git fi' dollahs fo' a big coon's skin, but one time I gots ten dollahs fo' a big jet black polecat wid long hair. Us'lly, eny-weah frum one tah three dollahs fo' a polecat, but I ain't nevah got mo'n fifty-fi' cent fo' 'pos'm. Don't mattuh' wid dis un', eny how, 'cause we gone makes a seat outtah it. Well, why don't we go see Luthah Ray? Dat wull gib us sumpin' tah do."

The two men started walking to the car. "Stay heah, Slick," ordered Quincy.

"Why do you call him Slick?"

"He ain't got no ha-uh tah speak of. Jest as slick as a ottah."

"By the way, what are we going to do at Luther Ray's?"

"You see," said Quincy, smiling as he noticed Ian continually scratching his forearm.

Eight

QUINCY DIRECTED Ian north onto Highway 1. *I've Got My Mojo Working* played on Ian's radio. "I know dat 'un. I huhd it play on a recuhd playah one time ovuh at Quo-tez's place. Muddy Watuhs, now *dat's* some blues player! Only mets 'eem whunce." Several miles north of Rosedale, a road sign informed Ian the men had reached the Gunnison community. Population, four hundred twenty-two. "We be at Gunnahson, now. Turn left heah." Ian drove west down the road, one of several thousand, dirt arteries meandering through the Delta flatland.

"I thought you said that you couldn't read," Ian quipped.

"Can't. I jest know weah we'z at, dat's all. Ain't got no idee whut dat sign we jest pass' say."

As the men traveled down the dusty, one-lane road, Ian could not contain his curiosity. "If you don't mind my asking, just *what* are we going to do at Luther Ray's?"

"I dun tole you, you see. I bin note-ah-sin you scratchin' yo' ahm ah lot."

"Oh, yes, I really don't know why."

"Luthah Ray got jest da thang tah gits rid o' it."

Technically, Luther Ray's wasn't a sharecropper's house, for Luther Ray was no longer a sharecropper. His Auntie Lela Mae had left the house, such as it was, to Luther before she died. In many ways, it looked like the typical sharecroppers' home: tiny, decrepit, sordid, leaky, and rarely supplied with utilities or bathrooms. As usual, the yard's only grass was sparse sedge, sprinkled with all sorts of antiquated tools that had been set to the side and forevermore neglected. Two abandoned cur puppies sniffed for victuals around an old mule wagon that was missing its two rear wheels and resting on a slack, barbed wire fence. Adjacent to the wagon, Ian noticed a small vegetable garden. Luther Ray's was what the blacks often called "tah-pa-puh" houses because of the ceilings sealed in tarpaper. They also were often called shotgun houses because all three rooms in the house were lined up behind each other so that if a shotgun were fired through the front door, the shot would go out the back.

"I thank he's heah."

Within a moment of hearing the men drive up in the car, Luther Ray Hodges exited his front porch door. "Hey, who you got wid'ya?"

"Awwh, jest somebody wantin' tah luhn sum blues. How ya' bin doin', Luthah Ray?"

Luther Ray dismounted the porch, meeting the men halfway. He was somewhat suspicious of a white visitor. The last time a white man came calling was when four lawmen arrested Luther's wayward son for murdering another black man over a woman of ill-repute.

"Awh, ah-ite, I guess. You?"

"Yep, can't cumplain. Gots eny smokes? I be out."

Luther Ray reached from his torn pocket to give Quincy one of his filterless Camels. He then struck a match and held it out for Quincy, while simultaneously keeping one eye on the stranger. Quincy had never betrayed Luther Ray in all of their years of friendship; yet, he couldn't figure out why he was with a young white man. The two men shook hands.

"Whin you gets ow-ah age, dah cott'n bosses thank you git too slow in dah fiels," Luther Ray began, as if he were instigating a response from Ian. Both black men chuckled.

"What is so funny?"

"Oh, nuttin' much," Quincy replied. "Whut dah white man don't know is, we may be ol', but we ain't no fool. We kin still out-wuck meny o' dem youngun's dey got cummin' in wuckin' fo' two dollahs a day, when we usetah git fifty cent fo' two hunded fifty pounda' cott'n a day. But, we fine's othuh thangs tah do, too." This instigated more snickers from the two black men.

"Yep," added Luther Ray, "dese days, men ow-ah age kin aw-most lib off our gahdin's. Sumtimes, we git a little change fo' playin' in dah juke jo-uhnts."

Quincy nodded his head in agreement to Luther Ray's every word. Luther Ray and Quincy were the same age and had been friends for several decades. Luther Ray stood six feet, one inch tall, but he weighed no more than one hundred and fifty pounds soaking wet. The fifty-five years of picking cotton had caused Luther Ray to stoop over a bit, making his lanky frame seem shorter.

"Whad y'all up tah t'day?"

Quincy explained to Luther Ray Ian's reason for visiting Rosedale. On occasion, the Southern colloquy was very difficult for Ian to comprehend. Sometimes Quincy recognized this and spoke slowly and clearly when chatting with the Englishman. But when Quincy and Luther Ray spoke with one another, it was an entirely different language to Ian. Their speech was unintelligible, impossible to decipher, and very unlike the English to which he was accustomed.

"He foun' me, way back in dah ol' levee boss' house off o' dah ol' Mah-tin Road. Dis mo'nin,' I noticed he bin scratchin' his ahm a lot, Luthah Ray."

Feigning detachment, Luther Ray was actually relieved to know Ian's reason for visiting. Smiling and nodding, he added, "Oh, *I* see why's you brought 'eem heah now. Got jest tha' thang fo' dat itch."

Luther Ray led the two men around back. A number ten washtub was centered in the back yard.

"Strip down," demanded Quincy.

"Huh?" asked Ian.

"Dat's ra-at, I said strip down. Take off dem ovah-alls an' enythang else you got on."

"You aren't serious. What's that in the tub?"

"Goat milk," replied Luther Ray. "Sweet milk dah best thang fo' whut you got, but ain't got eny ra-at now. Goat milk 'el do. Good thang I got sum goats, huh, Quincy?"

"Yep, sho' is," replied Quincy.

"How dreadful! I will *not* get into that tub. I will just see the nearest physician."

"Phah-zish-un?" Quincy asked. "You mean by dat dah neahist doctah, don't ya'? Okay din, stop wastin' my time. If'n you see-uh-us 'bout luhnin' dah blues tah da bess o' you abil-ah-tee, an' if'n you really do want me tah be yo' mentah as you calls it, den do what I says. Else, stop wastin' my time an' Luthah Ray's."

"Yes, you're right—again," replied Ian. Ian began to undress.

"We black folks 'roun' heah nevah really had no doctah tah speak of," Luther Ray added, "ceptin' whin dah white boss man on dah plantation thought it'd be in his bes' intrust tah git a doctah whin one o' us git sick. But mose o' dah time, we blacks jest had tah cum up wid owah own rem-ah-dees. An' we got one fo' yo' scratchin'."

"What do you think is wrong with me?"

"Ain't no doubt whut wron' wit choo," said Luther Ray. "You dun got yo'sef intah sum pois'n ivy."

Quincy nodded. "Yep, fo' sho'. Dah fust time I seed you, whin Slick be lickin' on ya', I seed a red blistah spot on yo' fo'ahm. 'Sho' 'nuff,' I say to myself, 'dat boy dun got intah sum poison ivy.' Whin you sleepin', you be leanin' up 'ginst a big vine. Dat vine fulla' poison' ivy."

Ian undressed and sat in the tub, knees up to his chin. "This isn't going to be easy; I can barely move in this contraption."

Luther Ray and Quincy could not contain themselves and burst out in laughter. "Me an' Luthah Ray gone go back 'roun' front. Bathe real good, now. Dat milk make you feel bettah." Ian had never experienced a bath in such a tight space, much less, one in goat milk. If his British friends were to see him now, he thought. Twenty minutes later, Ian returned to the front porch, where Quincy and Luther Ray were each holding a bottle of Falstaff beer.

"Well, how's ya' feel?" asked Quincy, smiling.

"Much refreshed. Much better than I thought possible."

"Milk do dat fo' poisn' ivy an' poisn' oak," said Luther Ray.

"But, don't you think it would be best if I could wear my own clothes now?"

"Nope," responded Quincy.

Ian heeded their advice and then asked, "Tell me, do you blues men get royalties from your songs?"

Luther Ray and Quincy both looked at each other, then toward Ian.

"What be dat?" asked Luther Ray.

"Royalties are monies that music industries give you for playing your songs. They go to the songwriters."

Luther Ray turned and looked at Quincy. "Quincy, you evuh huhd o' sech?"

"Nope."

"Well, if anyone has taken your songs and made records out of them, the royalties are rightfully yours."

"Heah dat?" exclaimed Luther Ray. "You'z could be rich, Quincy!"

Quincy asked skeptically, "What duz I have tah do tah git dese royalties?"

"Hire an attorney, for one thing. Then, I suppose, he would show you what to do next."

"An ah-tuh-nee? Well din, jest forgit it."

"Yes, but..." said Ian.

"I say, jest forgit it. Ain't no white man gone be my ah-tuh-nee."

"Quincy," interrupted Luther Ray, "Do you know whut you be sayin'?"

"Yep. I say forgit it. Eb'n if'n some ol boys *did* steal my songs an' move up no'th wid 'em, I ain't goin' no-we-ah. Dun tole you dat, Ian."

Ian observed that Quincy had called him by his given name for the first time.

"Well, thanks fo' dah smokes an' be-ah," said Quincy. "I reckon' we bettuh be on ow-ah way."

"Luther Ray, do you play the blues, too?" Ian asked.

Luther Ray peered over at Quincy. Quincy nodded. Luther Ray rose from his cane-seated chair, entered the house, and returned with a hand-held instrument Ian had never seen before.

"What the devil is that?"

"Dem be quills," replied Quincy. "Dah fust ones wadn't made no-we-ah 'roun' heah. Back in dah ol' country, ow-ah ancestahs in Af-ree-ka made dem. Some peoples call 'em panpipes. We mosely call 'em quills."

"May I look at those?"

"Sho'."

Ian carefully observed their simple yet clever construction. They were made from several hollow cane tubes tied together with pieces of bamboo fibers. The tubes were tied parallel and approximately eight inches in length. Quincy pulled his harmonica from his shirt pocket. "Any time I's headed ovah dis way, I brings dis," Quincy said. "Luthah Ray an' me sumtimz jest sit an' vent'late."

"Ventilate?" asked Ian.

"Yep, dat whut we calls it. We be lettin' off steam."

"Steam? I'm afraid I don't quite understand."

"What Quincy mean is, we be wuckin' fo' dah white man fo' so lone dat we seed many sah-ee scoundruhls. Dey treat us real bad. Not all o' 'em, but sum o' 'em. We can't talk back tah 'em, lest we want tah be strung up o' beat wid a pistahl o' sumpin'. So we jest takes it. Din, whin we gits home at night, we vent'late. You know, we let out ow-ah fuhs-tra-tion by playin' ow-ah blues." Quincy nodded sporadically as Luther Ray explained.

For the next hour, Luther Ray and Quincy played several blues tunes that Quincy had devised. Like thousands of times before, the duo lost all track of time. Playing music made them forget all their sorrows of the past. Ian began to notice that their music was greatly affecting him as well. He sat mesmerized, temporarily forgetting all about Deputy Purvis' mistreatment and about the day he would have to return to England.

"Gotsta' be abel tah make dah hah-mon-ee-cah talk back tah yah. Ain't dat ra-at, Luthah Ray?"

Luther Ray merely nodded.

"Amazing! Fantastic!" shouted Ian when the two men appeared to be finished.

"All us 'roun' heah who play dah blues gotsta' know how tah make some instra-mints. Not meny peoples 'roun' heah, 'speshallee dah yungun's cummin' up, kin eb'n play 'em."

"Where did you get the material to make these?" asked Ian, as he continued to examine the quills.

Both black men cackled again. "Dat be frum dah cane down in dah swamp," responded Quincy. "I show ya' sum time."

"Great! I would love to learn how to make and play the panpi— I mean, the quills."

"Might be back in a day o' two. We need tah let Ian meet Bessie Lee."

Luther Ray laughed. "Ah-ite. I thank we kin hanell dat," he added as he thumped a Camel into his yard.

They said their good byes. Dusk was settling in.

When the men got into the car, Ian asked, "Who's Bessie Lee?"

"You see," said Quincy, "you see soon 'nuff."

Nine

WHILE HEADING BACK TO Highway 1, Quincy listened quietly while the radio played *Evil (Is Going On)*. He was enjoying the radio tunes as much as Ian, and it became a custom of his to sit quietly while the blues aired on the radio. "Heah dat piano playin', don't ya? Man, I lacks dat sone. See dat place ra-at deah?" As they passed a long, straight driveway extending for more than three hundred yards, Ian beheld his first Southern plantation. "Dat be Mistah Mo'gensen's place. He own pritne-ah mose o' Bolivah County down dis way. We'll go up deah one o' dese days."

Ian struggled to understand the white Southern plantation owner's rationale for his treatment of black sharecroppers. Each time that Ian brought the subject up to Quincy, it only brought a terse "hmmph." Ian prodded no further when he detected Quincy's discomfort with the subject.

Arriving at Quincy's, the men rested on the porch. Katydids could be heard throughout the woods, interspersed with the cacophony from tree frogs and chirping crickets.

"Listen to that, Quincy."

"Yep, dat be katydids, rubbin' deir wings tah-ga-thuh. Dey wouldn't eb'n be heah if'n dah rivah didn't take a mean tuhn dah uthuh way. Since it tuhn dah uthuh way, wadn't no need in cuttin' dese trees. Dat's weah dah katydids an' locus stay, up in dah trees. I heah's a tree frawg, one o' two crickets, too."

"What are those tiny lights flying everywhere?"

"Lightnin' bugs. Dat be lightnin' bugs. Huhd 'em callt fi-ah flies, too."

"Quincy, how old are you?"

"Bone' in Augus', ninety eight. Don't know 'xactly what day."

"Do you have a family?"

Quincy arose and stepped into the house. Ian felt he had touched another sore spot with the blues man. Quincy returned with his guitar, and Ian waited desperately to see what Quincy would do next. "My mama an' papa both wuckt deah whole lifetime fo' Mistah Mo'gensen's daddy. Dey both dead and beh-eed not too fah frum heah."

"I notice that you don't use a plectrum to play."

"Say ag'in?"

"You know, a plectrum, a pick. You don't use a pick to play the strings."

"Oh, no, ain't nevuh hudh it callt a plectrum befo'. Lone time 'go, I used a piece o' bone dat had a hole in it dat fit my thumb jest ra-at. Lost it one day. So I figuhd I ma-at as well play wid-out one cuz I be losin' dah picks. Got usetah playin' wid-out. Bin lack dat evuh since. I knowd one blues playuh who uses a iv'ry pick. He to-ah op'n a piano tah git dah iv'ry out o' dah keys," Quincy added as he chuckled. "Uthah gitah playuhs use a piece o' metal fo' a pick, but I don't lacks 'em. Nawh, sho' don't. Din't hab no shouldah strap, eithuh, fuh yeahs; but a blues playah one night at a honky-tonk gib me his. Sayed I could hab it as lone as I keep playin' dat night. I played for two ow-ahs."

"Do you have any brothers or sisters?" asked Ian, as he swatted at a mosquito in front of his nose.

"Yep. At least, I *did*. Had seb'nteen brothuhs an' sistahs. I's thuh younges' o' all eighteen chilluns'. We all wuckt fo' eithuh Mistah Mo'gensen o' his son, Joonyah. Only ones left be Quo-tez, me, an' two sistahs who wuck fo' Miss Mo'gensen. Dey do whatevah she say, you know, make cone bread, quilts, wuck in huh gahdin, chop cott'n."

Quincy abruptly stopped talking about his family and took up his guitar and began singing.

Hahd times, dey always be,
Frum dis day tah etuh-nah-tee,
Hoein' an' choppin' all day lone,
Stoppin' tah eat Mama's cone pone...

Quincy then stopped just as abruptly as he had begun. "I recon' you fixin' tah axse me if'n I evuh had wife en chillins o' my own."

"Well, I wanted to. But if you would rath—"

"No, it be ah-ite. Dat's whut blues all 'bout. Makin' up songs 'bout yo' life an' dah hahd times dat cums wid it. Reckon' if'n I didn't know 'bout hahd times fust hand, wouldn't know how tah sing no blues."

Quincy paused momentarily before continuing. "Had a wife an' son once. One day, we be wuckin' in dah fiel'. Wife got tah feelin' sick. Soon, thah son did, too. Didn't have no doctah' on dah plantation tah take huh an' son tah. Typhoid got 'em. Dey be beh-eed next tah my folks an' othuh fam'ly membuhs up et Waxhaw. Hmmph, whin my wife an' chile die, Ol' Man Mo'gensen tole' me I could have dah day off fo' deah foo-nuh-rul. Next day dough, I had tah be back in dah fiel's, choppin'. Said dah cott'n wouldn't wait. Dat wuz in nineteen an' nineteen, jest aftah Wuhl Wah One." The song *Death Letter Blues* came to Quincy's mind:

I gotta lettuh dis mo'nin', I do,
You reckon' it read,
It say, Hurry, the girl you love is dead.

I gotta' lettah dis mo'nin,
Hmm, How do you reckon' it read?
You know it say, Hurry, Hurry,
On a count the girl you love is dead.
Oh, I grabbed up my suitcase,
Took out down the road.
When I got there, she was layin' on tha...

"Guess we oughta' git sum sleep," said Quincy.
"Okay. Can I freshen up a bit before I turn in?"
"Oh," said a surprised Quincy.
Ian began to wash in an old, white ceramic bowl sitting on a homemade dresser.
"Whew! Where's the hot water?"
"Oh, if'n you need *hot* watuh, I have tah git dah stove goin' wid sum fi-ah-wood."
"Just to wash up?"
"Hmmh, yep. You said you wuz willin' tah do whatevuh it take tah make you a bettuh blues play-uh."
Ian decided it wasn't as expedient as he had thought. "Well I suppose I will just wash with cold water. Is this water the same as we drank from earlier?"
"Yep, it too frum thuh crick. Gotsta' have sum buckets whin ya' stay out in dah woods."
"I see. Then, how do you keep food cold?"
"Hmmph, see dat deah?" asked Quincy, as he pointed toward an old icebox. "Whin's I kin, I git sum ice ovuh at Clevelan' o' Greenvahl. Don't nobody cum 'roun' Rosedale no mo' in ice truck. So, I's gotta' git a ride tah a big city jest tah git ice ese days. Din, I put dah ice in deah."
"Have you ever heard of a refrigerator?"
"Yep, seen one wunce, too. It wuz in dah back o' a pickup truck. I had tah ask whut it wuz," Quincy added with a smile.
"I see."
"The levee bosses put in dis sink, but dey nevuh git 'roun' tah diggin' dah well."
"I don't suppose there is any way you would have a telephone, would you?"
Quincy answered with a solemn stare; Ian got the message.
"Where do *I* sleep?"
"Heah, sleep on dat," answered Quincy, pointing to an old cot in one corner. Ian slumped down on the makeshift bed.
"What's dat noise?"
"Hmmh, you mean undah ya? Oh, dat jest be dah cone shucks settlin' down undah ya'. Dey's whut dah mattress made frum. Sumtimes, I use dry grass. But dis time o' yeah, I use cone shucks."

Quincy was about to blow out the kerosene lantern. "What the devil is that?" Ian asked, rising from the cot.

"Oh, dat be roaches. Don't eb'n thank 'bout killin' 'em."

"Why not?"

"You see." Quincy stood on the foot of the bed, reaching out and grabbing one roach, as the other one escaped. Quincy calmly set the roach in a spent kitchen matchbox. Quincy had glued a screen on one side of it. Then he followed the other roach to the other side of the room and caught it, placing it in the box.

"What, pray tell, will you do with those?"

"Sell 'em, if'n I don't use 'em fo' brim bait. You 'el see. Good night. Oh yeah, one mo' thang. See dat deah white ja-ah jest undahneath dah bed?"

"Yes. What is it?"

"Slop ja-ah. Use it if'n you needs tah go duh-in' dah night."

"To go?" Ian naively asked.

"Boy-ah, you really is a greenhone, ain't ya'? Eethuh use *it*, o' if'n you needsta', deah be dah outhouse in dah back."

"Oh, I got you." Ian quickly fell asleep.

Quincy remained awake, smoking his last Lucky Strike for the night. "Hmmh," snickered Quincy to himself, "Aftah a while, dat 'pos'm be wuckin' on Ian's stomach. Dat fo' sho'."

Later that night, Ian *did* need to go visit the outhouse. He found the matches and lighting the lantern, he walked around back. While sitting in the outhouse, Ian examined the close quarters and its construction. In one corner of this four-by-five wooden makeshift structure was a fragmented dirt dauber nest. Ian's attention was drawn to a Sears & Roebuck Catalogue. At least, it was part of one, for many pages had been ripped out. For a moment, he was confused. Why would an illiterate sharecropper need a catalogue, unless he wanted to look at the pictures? And, if he did, why were many of the pages torn out? When Ian failed to locate any toilet paper in the outhouse, he surmised the catalogue's purpose.

Ten

IAN WAS SLEEPING SOUNDLY the next morning. "Wake up, Ian, new day."

"What time is it?" Ian asked, as he turned slowly with squinted eyes.

"Don't ra-atly know. Prob'ly 'roun' fo'."

As far as Ian could remember, he had never seen four o' clock in the morning. "You can't be serious. It isn't even light outside yet."

"Hmmph. You hongry?"

"Pardon?"

"I say, is you hongry, you want sumpin' tah eat?"

"What are the choices? Or, *are* there choices?"

"No, 'fraid not. Jest dah usu'l. I got sum cone meal biskits wid mo'lasses. An' o' few pieces o' ham left frum Lovie Mae's last hawg I kilt fuh huh. I's outta' eggs."

Ian felt he had to do what Quincy suggested. Otherwise, he would be returning to Cambridge without accomplishing his goal. For a while longer, Ian would have to forget the comfort of home.

"Sounds fine."

"Okay, then I reckon' you bettuh' git up. Gone be daylight befo' you knows it."

Quincy's kitchen table had been left by levee bosses years before. It had served Quincy well and was used for many other purposes. Quincy set the plate before Ian, which consisted of two slices of smoked ham and three stale biscuits left over from the day before.

"Deah, eat up," said Quincy, with a short grin. Quincy enjoyed seeing Ian's varied expressions. Quincy knew that Ian was still surprised at how blacks in the Delta lived.

After breakfast, Ian asked, "Do you suppose, Quincy, I could take a bath? By the way, where *is* your bathtub?"

"Wait a few minutes whin it git lightah. Then I shows you."

"What are we going to do today?"

"Well, let's see. I reckon' we could go ovuh tah Quo-tez's gahdin. He halfway spectin' me t'day, anyways. His peas an' okra be ready 'bout now. An' probl'y sum uthuh vej-tah-bels."

The men eventually finished eating. "Well, I reckon' I kin show you my bathtub now. Cum' on. It's out back."

Ian followed Quincy around back, but the river's fog had not yet lifted. "This fog is as thick as I once saw six or seven years ago when I made a trip with my parents to London," Ian commented. "Over four thousand people died."

"Sho' nuff?" asked Quincy with great surprise.

"It's known as The Great London Fog. We couldn't see but two to three feet in front of us. Some died in accidents due to zero visibility, but others died due to the fog mixing with the smoke from the coal-burning stoves; they were asphyxiated from sulfur dioxide."

"Dey wuz as-fix-ee--?"

"-Ated; they were asphyxiated. It just means they suffocated. They couldn't breathe. London is notorious for its fog."

"Whut 'xac-lee is fog?" asked a curious Quincy.

"Really, nothing more than clouds at ground level. That's really all it is."

"Clouds? Down heah?"

"Yes. As long as the air at the ground is cool enough to reach saturation, fog will form."

"Hmmph, well, whud'ya' know. Dis heah fog us'ly be buhnd up by nine o' clock."

The men had made their way to the tub. "Deah's you go. Lucky fo' you I got sum hot watuh frum dah stove ra-at now. Else, you be takin' a bath in cole crick watuh."

Quincy added hot water from a pot he had carried out of the house. "Heah, I got sum P & G soap. It 'el do dah job."

"Why, it looks like Luther Ray's."

"Yep, it 'bout dah same."

Quincy returned to the house while Ian bathed. There were two reasons Ian did not complain about the tub: one, he preferred a bath of water over a milk bath any day; and, two, he knew that any time he complained, Quincy might call it quits. Ian finished his bath and returned to the house. Quincy was sipping a cup of coffee he had heated up on the cook stove. "Lack some?" asked Quincy, as he held out a well-used ceramic cup.

"No thank you, I don't drink that stuff." After a slight pause, Ian continued. "Uh, don't think that I am complaining, Quincy; but, do you suppose since I am going to wear your overalls that I could possibly wash them?"

"Don't see why not. We gits tah it dis aftahnoon."

Ian watched Quincy set the box of roaches on the car's floor-board. He did not bother to ask what their purpose was, but he was sure that Quincy would inform him at the appropriate time.

QUARTEZ QUARLES lived twenty-six miles away, near the small town of Shelby, Mississippi. Upon their arrival, Quartez was on his way to his garden with hoe in hand. Quincy introduced Ian to his brother and Ian held out his hand to shake Quartez'.

"I heared 'bout you whin I stopped at Happy's dah othuh day," said Quartez. "Sho' is strange."

"What is?" asked Ian.

"You cummin' all dah way frum Englan' ovuh heah," Quartez continued. "Mos' peoples tryin' tah git *outta'* dis Delta, but heah you is, visitin' it! Don't seem ra-at."

"Yes, I suppose it is illogical to most."

"Strange," said Quartez, "dat's all I gotsta' say 'bout it."

Quincy just smiled. He was already growing accustomed to Ian's British culture. "What row's dun bin pickt t'day?"

"Nun jest yet. I's jest got out heah."

"Ah-ite, din I'll show Ian how tah pick dese heah peas. Mose of 'em look lack dey ready tah be picked. Look heah, Ian; dese heah is whut we calls puhpil hull peas."

"Yes, I have heard of black-eyed peas," replied Ian, as if he thought they were one in the same.

"Dese heah ain't black-eyes," Quincy said. "Dey's pink-eye puhpil hull peas, an' dey's easy tah pick. All you gotsta' do is pick dah puhpil un's. Leave dah green uns fo' 'nuthuh day. Jest conc'ntrate on dah puhpil uns, ah-ite?"

"Yes, got it," replied Ian, as Quincy handed him a large croaker sack. Within fifteen minutes, all three men were sweating profusely in the hot August sun.

"Dis a croakah sack," Quincy said. "Used 'em meny times fo' cott'n. So, we don't throws it away whin we git through t'day. We 'el be usin' it in a month o' so in dah cott'n fiel's."

"Fo' sho', dah black man don't throw nuttin' away," added Quartez.

"Hey Quo-tez?" asked Quincy. "You got eny okra needs cuttin'? I know we can't leab it on dah stalk if'n it needs cuttin'. B'sides, we needs tah show Ian what it lack tah cut okra."

Both Quartez and Quincy smirked. Ian had learned that any time two black men began to snicker and talk unintelligibly, he was probably the topic of conversation. Ian picked approximately two hundred linear feet of peas. Having accomplished this milestone, Ian had halfway expected the brothers to congratulate him for his toil. "Greenhone, fo' sho!" shouted Quartez to his brother. "I see what's ya' mean now. He be slowuh dan a snail on Mundee mo'nin'."

"Okay, you ready fo' sum real sho 'nough itchin'?" asked Quincy. "It's a good thang we didn't throw out dat goat milk at Lutha Ray's, 'cause I got a feelin' you gone be needin' it 'gin," he said with a grin. "Now, if'n you 'el lissen' tah me an' Quo-tez, you be gittin' wise-ah. Fact is, I can't tell ya' nuttin' 'bout no book luhnin', dat's fo' sho'. Mos' black folk 'roun' heah can't, neethah. But we 'el show ya' whut it lack tah live po'. See, dis heah is whut we call okra. Sum white peoples call it okree. But if'n you don't watch out, it'll git dah best of ya', jest lack dat ol' poison' ivy you gots intah a day o' two back."

"Peach fuzz 'el do it, too," interjected Quartez.

"Lucky fo' you, you got lone sleeves on," Quincy added. "Dat 'el hep. What-evah you do, don't staht scratchin'. 'Cause if'n you do, an' you rub yo' eyes, well, you be wantin' tah jump in dat ol' pun ovuh deah," pointing to Quartez' shallow cow pond nearby. Ian ingested every word of advice from Quincy's lips. Quincy showed Ian how to cut the okra off the stalk with one of Quartez' knives. As Ian began to cut the okra stalks, the two brothers began to pick tomatoes, banana peppers and cantaloupes. After two hours of toiling in the garden with his back aching, Ian stopped for a break.

It was then that Ian heard something unlike anything he could ever recall. The black men were singing, but it was not typical singing. Nor was it like the singing at Mount Nebo Missionary Baptist Church. Ian was hearing his first field hollers. Quartez started, then Quincy joined in. The two men's voices flowed together smoothly.

Freedom! Freedom!
Freedom! Freedom!

Back in Cambridge, Ian had been trained professionally on the piano; so, he could easily identify good timing and harmony. He was amazed that such unison could come from two untrained cotton pickers of the Delta. They could not read a musical note or a letter of the alphabet for that matter; but they sang in such wonderful unison. And all of this was done while in the noonday sun and humidity. A strange feeling pervaded Ian Smythe. He knew that he had not experienced real suffering as many of the Delta blacks had. But he could at least empathize with their social status and way of life. Ian felt that he was ready to accompany them, so he began to sing as well, wondering what the brothers would think. The brothers looked up, but said nothing; they just kept singing. All three men were then singing one of the old field hollers that had been sung in that flat Delta soil for over one hundred years. Three hours and several hollers later, the okra, tomatoes, cantaloupes, banana peppers, and peas had been picked.

"Well, dat 'bout does it fo' t'day," said Quartez. "Heah, Quincy, y'all take dese." Quartez handed the men half of the day's pickings. "I don't need no mo' ra-at now, no way."

"Okay, thank ya' Quo-tez," answered Quincy. "Reckon' we best be on da' ro-ed. Gots lot tah show dis greenhone."

Both black men began to chuckle again as they said their goodbyes.

"Whew!" exclaimed Ian. "I can't wait to get home and rest for the remainder of the day."

"Rest? Hmmh, you fo' sho' can't do dat."

"What? I did my share."

"Yep, but dah day ain't ovah yet. Deah still be two ow-ahs o' sunshine." The men drove off from Quartez' home. Ian did not know what to expect next, although there was one thing of which Ian was sure: he could see that he really knew little about hard work. Yet, more was to come! On the way back to Quincy's, the men came to a small grocery store on Highway 1, near Gunnison. "Stop at dis sto'. We kin git sumpin' tah eat in deah."

Ian and Quincy had agreed earlier that Ian would buy everything at the store. Ian did not mind; they agreed it was only right. After all, Quincy hosted Ian at his house, and Ian felt that he was still getting the better end of the deal, anyway. Besides, Ian thought, where else could a greenhorn like I get such great lessons in the blues and, at the same time, receive such unique lessons about life?

Eleven

PARKER'S GENERAL STORE sold most of the basic essentials. While pulling into the lot, Ian noticed a large Nehi soda sign nailed to the west side of Parker's store. A new, shiny green Sinclair gasoline pump stood in the middle of the gravel lot. Few flies and mosquitoes made their way past the screen entrance door. Parker's store was stocked with all sorts of sandwich meat and goodies. The Parker's also sold washing machines and small furniture on time. A bait shop annexed the store on the east side.

"How y'alls be tee-day," said Quincy, as the two men entered the store.

"Hey, Quincy, how you doin?" asked Mrs. Billie Mae Parker.

Mr. Jim Parker spent most of his time in the back of the store, cutting or preparing bacon, sausage, hamburger, venison, and other Delta meat products. He despised having to help customers and only came to the front when Billie Mae asked him to help with someone's groceries or with some other need. Mr. Parker also kept the books and opened the store every morning. Mrs. Billie Mae would relieve him at the front counter at nine.

"Evah heared o' sardines?" asked Quincy.

"Yes, but I've never eaten them," replied Ian.

"Dat's fixin' tah change. Whadda' ya' say we git some RC's whiles we heah?"

"Will that be all?" asked Mrs. Billie Mae, as she began ringing up the tab.

Quincy looked toward Ian for approval before continuing his requests.

"Er," Ian began, "would you by chance have any chips?"

"Yes, we do," replied Mrs. Billie Mae, as she pointed to the potato chip rack.

"No, I mean fries. I mean French fries. We call them chips in England."

Mrs. Parker, embarrassed, frowned and replied, "Oh, no, we don't cook French fries here. Sorry."

"Uh, could we hab two packs o' Lucky Strikes, an' ah, I thank I 'el git sum mo' RC's fo' latuh. Y'all ain't outta' Garrett snuff, is ya', Miss Pahkuh? An' moon pies?" asked Quincy as he placed a spool of ten-pound monofilament line on the counter.

"No, Quincy, we got a new box of 'em jist the other day," replied Mrs. Billie Mae. Looking at Ian, Mrs. Billie Mae inquired surreptitiously, "Are you with Quincy?"

"Yass'um, he wid me," Quincy interrupted. "Mrs. Pahkuh, y'all still need sum mo' roaches fo' fish bait? I got sum out in dah cah."

"Sure, we still givin' a penny apiece for 'em."

Quincy stepped outside to the car and retrieved his box of roaches. "Mrs. Pahkuh, kin you cum out heah a minit' so'z we kin count dah roaches?"

Mrs. Parker counted as Quincy set the roaches---one by one---into an empty cricket box out front.

"Looks like you got seven of 'em. Come on back in, an' I'll pay ya' for 'em," Mrs. Billie Mae said as they re-entered her store. She paid Quincy for the roaches by counting out the three coins and placing them on the counter. "A nickel and two pennies." Ian wondered why Mrs. Parker set the three coins on the counter instead of placing them directly into Quincy's hand.

Ian then detected suspicion in Mrs. Parker. If Quincy had been riding in the back of one of Mr. Morganson's work trucks, she would have never taken notice. But Mrs. Billie Mae had seen Quincy get out of the front seat of Ian's car. Naturally, this would arouse any white person's curiosity. Ian didn't want to jeopardize his position with Quincy in any way. He thought that the less he said to any of the whites around there, the better. Ian paid for the items, and they left.

"Good heavens, seven cents? You caught those dreadful, disease-carrying pests for seven cents?"

"Hmmph, dat ain't nuttin'. I use tah git half a penny each fo' 'em."

"What is that spool of thread for? Are you planning to show me how to sew?"

"Dis ain't thread. Dis be fishin' line. One day, you'll see."

"One other thing, Quincy. Did Mrs. Parker intentionally set the three coins on the counter rather than place them in your hand?"

"Hmmph, dat jest dah way it be, Ian. Dat jest dah way it be."

No sooner had the two men headed south on Highway 1 than Deputy Sheriff Purvis and Bill drove in from the north.

"Didya' see that, Tom?" asked Mrs. Parker.

"What's that, Miss Billie Mae?" asked Bill.

"Didn't you see what just left outta' here headed south?" she asked again.

"No, sorry, ma'am, we didn't," answered the deputy. "Who was it?"

"Quincy Quarles," said Mrs. Billie Mae. "Y'all know Quincy. Anyway, he had some white boy drivin' 'eem 'round."

"Whatdya' say we head out after 'em?" asked Bill excitedly.

All three watched as Quincy and Ian headed south on Highway 1. "Naah," replied the deputy, as he removed his wire-framed sunglasses. "I thank we 'el jest wait-- till tonight. Looks like thah Council is gone tah have tah pay a visit tah Mr. Quarles' house."

Twelve

"TELL YA' WHAT," suggested Quincy, "Let's head back ovuh tah Lutha Ray's."

"Okay, whatever you think."

"Wait jest a minit!" Quincy exclaimed abruptly. "Stop dah car!"

"What? What happened?"

"Ra-at heah. See dat, look ah deah!" Quincy got out of the car and anxiously picked up three empty Pepsi coke bottles on the shoulder of the road. "See dat? I gits two cents ah piece fo' dem back at Pahkuh's." Quincy set them on the floor so that his feet could keep them from breaking. "Next time we go tah Pahkuh's sto', I git my two cent deposits on 'em. Drive on."

When they drove up to the house, Luther Ray came out, as was his custom.

"I thank it be time fo' Ian tah be intrahduced tah Bessie Lee," said Quincy, smiling.

Luther Ray returned the smile. "Ah-ite."

All three men went around back as several Rhode Island pullets scampered freely in the yard, looking for any morsel of food. Inside a makeshift holding pen stood Bessie Lee, all eleven hundred pounds of her. "Deah she be," said Luther Ray. "Bessie Lee, cum heah."

Bessie Lee approached the men. "Us black folk is known tah be muleskinnahs," said Quincy. "Usestah be, we used mules tah do all dah levee wuhk an' cott'n fiel wuck, too. Mules so im-po-tunt tah dah white man dat dey had a sayin': 'Kill a niggah, we'll hi-ah another'n. Kill a mule, *buy* another'n.'"

"Oh, come on, really?"

"Yep, fo' sho'," added Luther Ray. "You evuh heah o' Dred Scott?"

"No."

"Well, Dred Scott was a black slave livin''bout a hunded yeahs ago. He was set free, but den latuh, dah Soo-preme Cote say he can't have his freedum. Know why? 'Cause blacks wadn't seen as peoples, but as prop-eh-tee. Cote say Scott wadn't a sit-ah-sun, so he can't have his freedom. An' *dat* be dah truth." Ian stood there with mouth wide open, staring at Quincy. "Stuff lack dat still go on tee-day, too. Me, Quincy, an' Quo-tez all bin out in dah fields wid da fiel bosses, ca-eein' dey whips an' pistols on dey hips, ridin' up high on dey hosses."

"Well, Luthah Ray, why don't we show Ian sumpin' 'bout wuckin' dis heah mule?" suggested Quincy.

"Ah-ite."

Quincy grabbed the muzzle and started to put it over Bessie Lee's face.

"What's that for?" asked Ian.

"Can't have huh eatin' dah crops in dah rows whin she be wuckin'," answered Luther Ray.

Luther Ray led Bessie Lee out of the pen and into his garden. "We's gone hook up dah side harruh. It gone git dah wild grass an' weeds outta' middle. Same time, it be air-atin' dah dirt. Now, let me tell ya' 'bout dis heah mule, Bessie Lee. She be a good mule. Smatah dan eny hoss. Jest keep huh steady. Let me show you how fust."

Luther Ray took Bessie Lee up one row of his garden to loosen up the dirt, returning down the next row. Resting under a small cedar tree for shade, Quincy began to munch on sardines and a moon pie. He could not have been happier, seeing a white man try to do what he had been doing for nearly sixty years.

Luther Ray continued to show Ian how to lead Bessie Lee. "Dah best ways I know tah keep a straight line is tah set yo' eyes at a mahk, maybe a tree o' sumpin' way off down deah an' keep yo' eyes on it. Dat way, you can row a straight line. See dat white oak wid dah low lims deah?" Luther Ray asked, pointing. "Keep yo' eyes on dat. Den, whin you tuhn 'roun', fine' sumpin' down at dat row, too."

Both muleteers were enjoying seeing Ian in his first attempt to plow with Bessie Lee. In all of their years of working these brawny creatures, they had never seen a white man work with one. On a return trip down one row, the side harrow got caught on a root, slowing Bessie Lee to a sudden halt. The momentum thrust Ian into the handle of the harrow, knocking the breath out of him. After one hour of working Bessie Lee, Ian dropped to the ground. "Please, can I take a break?" begged Ian to the men. "My hands!" he exclaimed, looking at his palms. "They are hurting!"

"Reckon' so," said Quincy, with his usual grin.

"You gonna' git blistahs now," chuckled Luther Ray, "but I jest want ya' tah know whin we wucked mules, we wucked from sunup tah sundown. We used to call it 'Frum Can't see tah Can't see,' 'cause we would be out in dah fiels befo' sun risin' an' aftah it go down. Only break we got was lunch. Mules knowed whin it be lunch time. Dey jest stop pullin' 'roun' lunch time. We'd stop an' eat a moon pie o' sahdines fo' a foo minutes, an' den boss man say, 'Let's git back tah work'."

Ian listened with sympathetic ears, but he was certainly glad to see the work come to a halt.

"Mine if I git a few eggs befo' we go?" asked Quincy. "Look lack yo' yahdbuhds puttin' out dah eggs."

"Naawh, go 'head 'n git all you need," replied Luther Ray. Quincy removed his hat and put in eight eggs. Soon, Quincy and Ian were saying their good byes to Luther Ray. Little did the men know that the White Citizens Council was planning to pay them a visit that very night.

Thirteen

DARK HAD SETTLED by the time the pair arrived at Quincy's place. Ian slumped down on the porch. He had never experienced such soreness in his neck and hands. The blisters on his hands were intolerable. He assumed that Quincy would have a homemade remedy for all of his aches. Three hours later, the men were still sitting on the porch. Quincy tarried on the porch because that was his nightly ritual, but Ian stayed because he was too tired to move.

Rising from his favorite sleeping spot, Slick began to growl as he stared in the direction of Ian's car. "What is it? What is it, Slick?" Quincy whispered, as the coonhound continued to snarl. "Whoa, bo-ah. Prob'ly a coon."

"Did you see that?" Ian asked anxiously, as he quickly arose from his seat.

"Whadya' see?" asked a wide-eyed Quincy.

"I'm not sure, really. Close to my automobile, I don't know, it looked like a light from a flashlight or another vehicle. I couldn't tell for certain, but I no longer see it."

Slick lit off the porch just as he had done many times before when he was hot on the trail of a coon, opossum, or some other small animal. Quincy had always heard that the Delta woods were occupied by bears and panthers which had swum the Arkansas or Mississippi; but he had never personally seen either animal. That was part of the reason Quincy rarely entered the woods without his loaded twelve-gauge shoutgun.

"I am quite certain I saw a light of some kind," added Ian.

Quincy rose from his chair. "Sumpin' ain't ra-at, I kin tell ya' dat," he whispered. Quincy glared in Slick's direction as the dog crept near Ian's car and just out of sight. "Slick be defendin' his teh-ah-to-ee. Thang is, don't know whut frum jest yet." Then Quincy and Ian heard a single shotgun blast followed by a loud yelp from the hound. Then there was silence. "Uh-oh," remarked Quincy.

"What? What is it?"

"Dat ain't no coon huntahs. We got cump'nee," warned Quincy. He insinctively grabbed his shotgun. "I thank they's dun kilt Slick."

"What are we going to do?"

"Quick! We's gotsta' be aw-ful-lee quite," whispered Quincy. Grabbing the flashlight on the porch, Quincy led Ian to the side of the house and through a patch of pines. "Nobody knows dis heah but me."

"Knows what?" Ian quickly asked.

"'Bout dis heah," Quincy said, as he pointed to the ground. "Dis sto'm sheltah. Git inside."

Quincy quietly lifted a rotten pine limb that had fallen on the shelter's door. Just before entering the underground security, they turned and looked back toward the house. Quincy and Ian saw several men attired in white robes. Quincy whispered, "We bes' git in. Dey ain't seed us yet. But dey know we's heah sumweah." The men climbed down the rotten stairsteps of the spiderweb-infested shelter.

Ian's fear was beginnning to show. "What could they possibly want with *us*?"

Quincy lifted the door ever so quietly, for the robed intruders were approximately two hundred and fifty feet away. "Hmmph. I'z pritty sho' dey dun got wuhd dat a white boy bin down in dese woods. Dey's be dah White Sit-ah-cins Council."

"Who?" asked a puzzled Ian.

"Bettah' known as dah KKK. I knows you hudh ah dah Klan."

"But, what do they want? If they have harmed Slick, they may want to harm us."

"Yep, o' at least skeer ya' an' me. Who know whut dey ma-at do tah me, maybe strang me up on a oak lim' 'roun' heah. If'n dey don't strang me up, dey gone sen' me tah dah pen-ah-ten-sha-ree. Dat be Pahch-mun. Pahch-mun State Pen-ah-ten-sha-ree. 'Bout fo' yeahs 'go in a town called Money, a black teen-a-juh whistled at a white wom'n. Foun' 'eem few days latuh in dah Tallahatchie Rivuh. Had a cot'n gin fan tied 'roun' his neck. Huhd dat fifty thousan' black folks went an' viewed his body at a chuch whin his mama taken him back tah Ch'cago. She open dah caskit up so's ev'ybody could see 'eem."

The robed men's leader then made himself known. "Hey, Quincy! We know you heah someweah. And that white boy, too. I reckon' he didn't learn his lesson a couple days back. So, listen up, both of ya'. We don't want no trouble heah in Rosedale. We gone keep it that way, too. You heah me, boy? They might do things dif-uh-ent weah you come from, but that don't matter heah in Mi'sippi. We ain't gone let no com-mu-niss or Jew cum in heah an' stir thangs up. Now, we will give you one mo' chance. But after that, well, we might just have tah make an example of you, boy. Leave thah cuhluhd folks tah theirselves. Whites don't frat-uh-nize with thah nigra's 'roun' heah. If we git one more r'port that you are still messing with thuh blacks, well, the lesson you dun had won't compare tah thah next one you gone git! You hear me, Quincy? If we have tah come back, we gone buhn this place down."

"His voice sounds familiar to me," Ian whispered.

"Sho' 'nuff?"

"I'm quite sure I've heard it before. It has a distinct Southern drawl."

The robed men turned and left, while Quincy and Ian remained in the shelter. Upon hearing the men's vehicles' engines start up, Quincy slowly exited the shelter, with Ian following closely behind. Quincy and Ian caught glimpses of two pickup trucks' headlights through the woods. But where was Slick, each wondered. Quincy could not wait until daylight; the anxiety was too much to bear. He had to know what happened to his canine friend. He and Ian walked out to the trucks' track impressions.

"I've got it, Quincy! Now I remember where I've heard that voice before! I'm sure the white robed speaker was Bill. He was with Deputy Purvis after I left Happy's church. Yes, I'm quite certain that was Bill."

"Hmmph."

"Do you know him?"

"Yep, I knows 'eem. Thank his lass name be Allbritton. In dah daytime, he hides behin' dah law, lack a cow-uhd. But at night when they's got theah hoods on, he lacks tah be dah leadah. He be a racis' if I evuh knowd one."

Quincy soon found Slick a few feet away—dead. "Eight yeahs! Eight yeahs I had dis dog! Look how he gotta' die!"

"My, how dreadful! How can anyone hate another race like this?" asked Ian.

Quincy did not acknowledge Ian. Ian had grown accustomed to many of Quincy's mannerisms. If he asked something once and Quincy never replied, he knew to just let the matter go. Eventually, Quincy mumbled, "Leab 'eem heah. I gits 'eem t'moh-uh mo'nin', b'fo' dah buzzuhds fine 'eem." The two men walked back to the house and stopped on the porch. Quincy remained silent, needing the time to mourn. He trudged into the house and returned with his harmonica. Sitting down in his favorite spot on the porch, he began to play several blues tunes that Ian had never heard before. It seemed to Ian that Quincy came up with different songs quite frequently. It was as if he made the song up as he played on the porch.

Many thoughts were racing through Ian's mind as he sat listening to Quincy play. He thought, "How could one race be so hateful? Why take out vengeance on a dog? Had it always been this way? And what am *I* going to do about it?" Little by little, day by day, Ian started recognizing racism in the Southern Delta. He had overheard his first hints of racism when the two brothers at the airport discussed long hair and colored people. Ian had read about bigotry in his safe haven of Cambridge, four thousand miles away. He soon found that the Civil War had not erased bitter hatred nor brought the two races together in harmony. It merely exacerbated the issue. If the tension between the two races had not been removed by now, then apparently, it may never be.

Quincy sang and played his harmonica and fife for the next two hours, while Ian tried to sort through his mixed feelings. He realized how privileged he was to be there, learning from the master of blues. He sympathized with Quincy for losing Slick in such a way. Such is the life of a Southern black laborer, Ian thought.

THE NEXT MORNING, Ian awoke, only to find that Quincy was gone. He was not on the porch or around back. Ian looked straight ahead in the distance toward his car. Quincy was returning with a shovel leaning on his right shoulder. Bits of fresh dirt slowly fell from the knees of his overalls. "I've moved a lotta' duht fo' dah white levee bosses, but I jest moved my las'." Ian realized Quincy was referring to Slick's burial, but he knew of no words to console him. Ian was beginning to see why the Delta musicians deal with their losses by singing the blues. It was useless, and sometimes detrimental, to complain to the white man about them.

"Whad ya' say let's go down tah dah swamp?" suggested Quincy.

"Yes, whatever you think. Why are we going there?"

"Cut sum cane."

"Cane? I don't understand."

"Deah be two thangs I lack tah do whin I feel down lack dis. One be tah play dah blues on dah po'ch. Dah uhthah is tah go fishin'. We gots tah go tah dah swamp tah cut cane tah use fo' fishin' poles."

The morning's grass was still saturated with dew. Quincy grabbed his matchbox from the kitchen and proceeded to show Ian how to catch grasshoppers in the sage. "If'n you see anythang--roach, cricket, grasshoppah--grabs it an' put it in heah. We gone need all 'em fo' bait." After twenty minutes of scrabbling and scrambling in knee-high grass, the men had caught thirty-eight insects, the majority of which were grasshoppers and crickets. There wasn't enough space to pack all of them in the single kitchen matchbox, so Quincy gingerly stuffed several into his front pockets. One mole cricket was caught and crammed into the kitchen box along with many of the others.

Several feet away stood a small patch of bamboo, which many locals inaccurately referred to as cane. Quincy drew his two-foot, dull-bladed machete from its sheath that was attached to his belt. After several strokes of the arm, Quincy pulled out two stalks and began to clean all excess grass and leaves from them. "Dese wuck pritty good, I thank. Whin you pickin' out which cane tah cut, look fo' one sim'lur tah dese. It need tah be limbah, but not *too* limbah. I lacks dah bream tah be ab'l tah pull hahd. Ain't no fun if'n you use a stiff pole. But if'n it be too limbah, it break, 'specially if'n a cat git on dah line." He then pulled the spool of line out of his back pocket and tied on ten-foot pieces to the tip of each bamboo pole. Quincy then broke off two twigs nearby from a hickory and tied them on as quills. "Sumtimz, whin I kills a tuh-kee o' crow, I use dey wing fo' quills." Reaching into his shirt pocket, Quincy showed Ian a small pack of one-ought bream hooks. "Dese look small, but it all we need fo' bream. If'n a catfish git on dah line, I could be in trouble. I seed 'em straight'n dah hook befo'."

Ian followed Quincy like poults in single file behind the mother hen. Ian thought of the events that had transpired since he had left his homeland. Never, in his wildest imagination, did he think his quest for the blues would take him down a narrow path through a Delta swamp, catching grasshoppers in the wet grass and cutting bamboo along the way. After a short trek through briars and two small creeks, the men reached the slough. "Dis heah be a slough. We gone fish ra-at heah. Dis is one o' my fa-vuh-ite sloughs. By dah way, Ian, you evuh fisht befo'?"

"No, I'm afraid not."

"Well it ain't dat hahd. Takes gittin' useta *an'* it kin take pashunts, cuz dey ain't always bitin' lack peoples be wantin' 'em tah. Dat's jest paht o' it. Hep me relax, git away frum dah boss man ev'y whunce in a while." Quincy located his favorite spot about halfway around the slough.

Sloughs were overflows from the great river. When the Mississippi rose above the levees, the water would quickly find the lowest spots in the flatland, bringing the variegated species of fish with it. Catfish, gar, carp, bluegill, black bass, white bass, smallmouth, and white perch were the most common freshwater species to find their way into the hundreds of sloughs and lakes. After the river crested, the water in these low spots would remain. Seven years before, at this same fishing hole, Quincy had caught a fish that he did not recognize. He took it to Mr. Parker at the general store, where a Vicksburg Military Park employee, who happened to be buying fuel there at the time, identified it as a ganoid sturgeon.

Quincy removed one of the grasshoppers from his matchbox and adeptly stuck the hook's barb into its head and thorax, causing it to protrude from its abdomen. "I duz it lack dat so he's live longuh, you know, make 'eem squhm on dah hook as lone as I kin, so he's kin ahtrack a bream o' sun puch, maybe a crappie. In uh-lee sprang, jest aftuh we plants ow-ah gahdins, dah bream be beddin'. Dat whin dey all gits close tah-ge-thuh an' spawn. If'n dah watuh real sha-luh, you kin see dah beds. Dey look lack whe-ah a cow bin in deah, stompin' 'roun'. I kin smell 'em, too. Gots tah have a nose fo' it, o' you won't know whut you be smellin'."

Ian could not force himself to gouge that first insect with the hook's barb. Quincy reminded Ian of his oath to do *whatever* it took to learn the blues. That was all the necessary motivation Ian needed to bait his own hook. After several minutes of fishing, Ian checked his bait's status and accidentally hooked a low overhead cypress limb. Quincy showed Ian how to prevent that from recurring. Three minutes later, Ian's quill went under the surface of the water. "Deah he is; pull 'eem up; not too hard do'; you might snatch it frum his mouth. Easy, you kin do it." After applying Quincy's fishing advice, Ian finally landed the twelve-ounce bream. "Dat a *real* good 'un."

"That was fun! Now, what shall we do?" asked Ian, excitedly.

"Puts 'eem on dis streen-gah. We *fo' sho'* ain't gone let 'eem go. I kin tell ya' *dat*." Unlike most of the white fishermen, Quincy had never owned a tackle box. He didn't mind; the lighter he could travel, the easier it was. But this required him to carefully stuff his pockets with all that he needed for the fishing trip. He removed his stringer from the same pocket from which he had retrieved his bream hooks. The white man's stringer was made of chain, with individual hooks clamped together, similar to a safety pin. Quincy's stringer was unique: a five-foot piece of cotton bale twine. On one end of the stringer, Quincy had tied a home-made piece of metal approximately six inches long and an eighth of an inch in diameter. It had a sharp point, enabling Quincy to jab the fish through the bottom lip. "Sum peoples stick deir streen-gah all dah way through dah gills an' out his mouth, den throws 'em in dah watuh till dey git ready tah leave. Not me. I thank dey live longuh an' stays freshah 'til I be ready to go home by stickin' 'em in dah bottom lip, 'cept fo' white puch. Deir lip be too soft. I stick dem through dah gills." Quincy and Ian fished for two more hours until all signs of nibbling had ceased.

"Whad ya' say let's go see dah Mo'gensen's?" suggested Quincy. "I huhd Mistah Mo'gensen gone be needin' sum hep soon."

"Very well."

Quincy let Ian carry the stringer of fish. For whatever reason, Ian felt very proud to carry the fish: seventeen bream, two small bass, and one four-pound channel cat. "This stringer is getting heavy. I won't be disappointed when we finally return to the house."

"Hmmph, reckon' you won't. It ain't too much mo' tah go." Ten minutes later, they were back at the house. "Okay, now cum dah fun paht." Quincy entered the house, returning with a spoon, filet knife, a pair of pliers, and a bowl. For the next forty-five minutes, Ian learned how to spoon a fish's scales, nail a catfish to a tree to remove its skin, and then gut the fish. Ian kept reminding himself that all this learning about black Southerners' everyday lives would help him to help play the blues. That was his motivation, his drive to continue. "I'z almose outta' ice; so let's take dah fish ovuh tah Luthah Ray's later," suggested Quincy. Ian didn't mind--*anything* to be rid of the smelly fish!

WHILE GETTING BEHIND THE WHEEL, Ian looked over to the right side of the car. Just off the road, a makeshift cross stood next to a freshly-dug grave. The sticks which formed the cross were tied together with small vines of a tree. Quincy gave a glance over at the grave, but he said nothing. As they rode away, *When My First Wife Left Me* played on the radio.

Without Ian's prodding, Quincy offered, "I thought abouts hoboin' on dah Illinois Central once—dat's a railro-ed dat cum through dese pahts—tah play dah blues up no'th an' make sum money an' git outta' dis place, but decided 'ginst it whin I began tah thank 'bout dah crowds an' ghosts."

Soon the men arrived at the Morganson Plantation. The plantation had been in "Junior" Morganson's family for six generations. Ian had not seen such splendor in the Delta. Driving down the taintless driveway, Ian beheld the massive live oaks that had been meticulously planted a century before. Such neat order to the trees, carefully stationed in equal distance from one another, and Spanish moss suspended from many of the boughs. And there was the antebellum mansion, situated at the end of the long entrance road in regal beauty, with its hipped roofs, dormers, Doric pillars, white-painted brick, and a wrap-around balcony. Next to the Queen's Palace in London, this was the most splendid residence Ian had ever viewed.

"Antebellum," the Latin term for "before war," was the name associated with these large Southern estates. Many were established throughout the South during the thirty years before the Civil War. More than half of America's millionaires in the 1850s lived between New Orleans and Natchez, with the latter boasting over five hundred millionaires--second only to New York City's millionaires. Millionaires of that era wanted others to know of their wealth; and the mansions were built to impress their Southern aristocratic, socialite friends.

As they approached the white three-story mansion, Quincy commented, "Dis house didn't git touched in dah Civil Wah. Far as I know, it be one o' a veh-ee foo dat din't. All uthuhs burnt tah dah groun' o' jest fell outta' neglec."

Quincy's sister was sweeping off the back porch when the men got out of the car. "Hey, Quincy, whad you be doin' up heah?" asked Dovie Ruth.

"Hey, not too long back, I huhd Junyah gone be needin' sum hep 'roun' heah, eb'n do' dah cot'n crop ain't come in yet. Dovie Ruth, dis here be Ian Smythe—frum Englan'."

"Pleased to meet ya'. Yep, Quincy, I huhd Junyah put out dah wuhd he gone be needin' sum hep 'roun' heah."

"Yep, but deah be 'nuthah' reason we be heah t'day," Quincy said.

"Oh? What dat be?" Ian was just as curious as Dovie Ruth.

"Well, Ian got his fust 'speh-ee-ents wid a mule yest'dee. Bessie Lee—you know, Lutha Ray'smule—well, Ian gotsta' so' neck now. I told 'eem I got jest dah thang tah hep 'eem git rid o' it."

Dovie Ruth just smiled. "Ah-ite. You be talkin' 'bout dah hogs?"

"Yep. You ready, Ian?"

"I suppose so."

"Good. Now, don't fo'git, you say you gone do whatevah I say. Ra-at?"

"Yes," Ian replied reluctantly.

"Din come on. I's fixin' tah intra-doos you tah sumpin' new."

Quincy had worked for decades at the Morganson Plantation. He and Junior had a mutual agreement. Any time Quincy heard that Mr. Morganson needed some help, he would come by to check on it. Mr. Morganson—"Joonyah," to all of the blacks--was very familiar with the Quarles' family as well. Many of Quincy's ancestors had worked for his father and grandfather. Quincy led Ian around to the side of a large, two-story barn. A small herd of Durrock hogs was inside a rectangular pen. Other than a county fair he once attended in Cambridge, Ian had never been that close to swine before. In one particular section, Quincy pointed to a large puddle of mud and water. "You's gotsta' git down in dat mud."

"Are you quite certain, Quincy, that this is necessary?" asked Ian.

"Lack I tole ya' ahready, we gots rem-uh-dees fo' mose eny-thang. Fo' a crook neck, you's gotsta' git down in dat mud weah da hogs bin rubbin'. Rub yo' neck in dah mud real good."

Ian wanted to get this over with as soon as possible. He had already learned that he had to do as Quincy said, or else...Ian opened the gate and slowly knelt down, while Quincy and Dovie Ruth watched. "Dat's ra-at, jest git down deah. Dem's Durrock hawgs. Fine' eatin'. Dey 'el move ovuh as long as you ain't gittin' too close whin dey gots little un's. Eb'n dah lit'l un's got teeths. Dem sows jest as soon kill ya' whin dey pro-tectin' dey little un's."

Ian proceeded to rub his neck in the mire. Never in his wildest imagination did he think he would ever be waddling in the mud like a pig. What would his family and friends think of him back home if they could see him? Was learning to play the blues *really* worth it? Was he serious when he told Quincy that he would do *whatever* he needed to learn the blues? "Am I doing this right?" he asked.

Smiling, Quincy replied, "Yep. You doin' ah-ite. I reckon' dat be 'nough. Cum on outta' deah."

Ian was covered in mud from head to toe. "Now what? I suppose you are about to inform me that I have to stay in these dreadful clothes the rest of the day, right?"

"Naawh. Dovie Ruth gone show ya' how tah clean dem clothes now."

As Ian helped himself out of the mud, Quincy shouted, "Wait jest a minit'!"

Ian looked over his left shoulder. "What?"

"Don't panic, but you bess be gittin' outta' deah. Dat bo' hawg is gibbin' you dah look. Don't look at 'eem in dah eyes." As Ian looked over his left shoulder, an eight-hundred pound boar hog was staring and standing, almost waist-high. His grunt was unlike anything Ian had ever heard, and his terrifying two-inch tusks jutted from both corners of his mouth. Ian likened the potential duel to a matador and his first bull, with one exception: Ian had no sword! Without further ado, Ian quickly ran and escaped through the gate.

Dovie Ruth began to laugh. "Come on, I shows ya' now." Dovie Ruth led Ian around to the back of an adjoining shed. "I's gone show ya' how tah wash dem clothes."

"I have some more clothes in my vehicle. Might I wear them while we are washing these overalls?"

"Sho' can," Dovie Ruth answered.

Ian retrieved a shirt and pair of his pants from the car. Meanwhile, Quincy leaned against a post of the shed, smoking on a Lucky Strike.

"Where do I change?" asked Ian.

"Go back behin' dah barn," Dovie Ruth replied.

Ian heard someone from the back porch call out, "That won't be necessary. Let 'eem come up here!"

Dovie Ruth looked toward the direction of the house. "Yas'um, Miz Winahgene," replied Dovie Ruth. Dovie Ruth walked Ian to the back porch of the house.

"He can come in and wash up first," said Mrs. Winogene Morganson. Smiling at Ian, she said, "I didn't think you wanted to put clean clothes on until you had washed up."

"You're very kind. And, you are correct. I would love to be back at Quincy's taking a bath first."

"Come on up here. Lena will show you where to go to take a bath. She's in the kitchen. Lena! Oh, by the way, I'm Mrs. Winogene Morganson."

Ian replied, "Hello, I am Ian Smythe."

Looking at Lena, Mrs. Morganson insisted, "Lena, show Mr. Smythe the bathroom."

"Yas'um, Miz Winahgene," Lena replied, as she exited the back screen door. "Hey deah, I's Lena Stokes. I be's Quincy's sistah."

"Hello to you, too. I am Ian Smythe."

Dovie Ruth remained outside with Quincy while Lena showed Ian the way inside the mansion.

Lena was a large black woman, approximately seventy years of age. Tied around her rotund waist was a large white apron sprinkled with bits of meal from the morning's breakfast. Her hair was wrapped with a light blue kerchief.

"Pleased to meet you," Ian responded. "Did you say, Stokes?"

"Dat's ra-at, I ma-eed inta dah Stokes' family fo' tee fi' yeahs 'go. Husban' wuck heah, too. Dovie Ruth, she still be a Quolz. She ain't nevah ma-eed an' nevah had chillun's. Me, I gots thuh-teen. All but one wucks heah frum time tah time." Lena led Ian down the main hall to the bathroom. Ian admired the beautiful heart pine floors, antiques, and paintings from Europe. "Deah's you go."

"Thank you, Lena," said Ian.

"Miz Winahgene prob'ly be 'roun' whin you git out."

"Thank you," Ian responded rather happily. Looking down at the white, cast iron tub with claw feet, Ian added, "I haven't seen a *real* bathtub since I left Memphis."

"Yep, reckon not. Dis un' be impoh-ted all dah way frum France." Lena smiled and returned to her kitchen chores.

Ian began running his water. "Finally!" Ian thought to himself. "Hot water and inside plumbing! Oh, how I have missed it! *And*, I can stretch out my legs!" As Ian lay there in the tub, a wave of guilt began to engulf him. "Why should *I* get this special privilege of taking a bath inside? These people don't even know me. And yet, Quincy was not afforded the same privilege!"

While bathing, Ian dried off and put on clean clothes. Making his way down the luxurious corridor, a rather unique appliance attracted his attention: a 6-volt battery AM radio sitting on an antique maple table. As he inspected the radio closely, Ian made a commitment to himself: one day, he would purchase one of these for Quincy.

Mrs. Morganson was standing at the back door as if she were waiting to speak with Ian. "Well, Quincy told me a little about you while you were bathin'. After talking to him, I guess the thing to do right now is let Dovie Ruth show you how to wash those clothes. I'll talk to you ah-gin when you get through with the washin'."

Ian waited for Dovie Ruth to lead him back to the side of the barn.

"Heah we go," Dovie Ruth said.

"But don't the Morganson's have a washing machine?"

Dovie Ruth laughed. "Dat be fo' *dem*. Not us fiel wuckuhs. Yep, she uses sto' bought soap. Dis wash tub an' bluin' water an' homemade soap, dat whut we mosely uses. Heah, I'z show you how tah use dah scrub bo'ad. Din, we use dah uthah tub tah rinse 'em in."

Ian tried his hand at it as Quincy made his way back to Ian and Dovie Ruth. He did not want to miss Ian's latest experience with what blacks had always known.

"Dis ain't nuttin," added Dovie Ruth. "Whin I have tah wash ow-ah bed linens an' clothes, I puts dem in dat deah i'un wash pot. I boils dem till dey good an' hot. Den I stirs dem wid a stick."

Ian just watched and listened. He kept thinking that he would eventually find something in common with these Delta blacks. But not yet; it was so very different from that which Ian was accustomed. It was just as Quincy had told Ian the first time they met. It really *is* different here, set in isolation from the rest of the world.

"I know's you dun takin' a bath," Quincy said, "but if'n you wants tah keep luhnin' 'bout how tah play dah blues bettah, din follah me." Ian thanked Dovie Ruth for the washing lesson and followed Quincy. Ian was led to another garden. But this one looked different from Quartez'. Ian stared down several rows. It was hundreds of times larger! What lay before Ian boggled his mind. As far as his eyes could see, there were protracted rows of watermelons.

"Dis be whut Mistah Mo'gensen needed sum hi-ahd hep fo'. We fixin' tah gathuh sum wah-tuh-mel-ens." Throwing down the butt of his Lucky Strike, Quincy continued, "Heah, let's staht down dis row. Dey ain't *all* ready tah pick."

"How do you know?" Ian asked.

"Sum peoples jest *thank* they know sumpin' 'bout pickin' me-luns'. But dey don't'; dey be pickin' sum dat ain't ready jest yet." Quincy leaned over and thumped one. "You gotsta' thump 'em. Den you list'n. Dis un' heah, it be ready 'cause dah sound be jest ra-at. Since you have a mus'cal e-ah la-ack me, you prob'ly kin tell, too, whin it be ready. Sum peoples ain't got dah mus'cal e-ah tah know whin dey be ready. Heah, you try it."

Ian thumped a melon that he suspected was ready. "Yes, I see what you mean. I think this one is ready."

"You ra-at!" Quincy exclaimed, with a surprised smile. "Deah be utha ways tah tell. Fo' instence, see dis heah pigtail?" as Quincy pointed to the melon's tendril. "If'n it be dry while dah res' ah dah leaves an' dah vine look good, it be ready tah pick. 'Nuthah way tah tell is weah deh melon be sittin'. If'n dah spot be yellah, it be ready. If'n it be green o' white, don't pick it. It ain't ready jest yet." Ian had always been a studious learner in school. He listened to Quincy's every word just as intently as he had as a student. Ian never dreamed that some of his greatest lessons would be in the Mississippi Delta with a few black laborers. As instructed, he climbed into the work truck while Quincy and a few other laborers threw the melons up to him.

"Where are all of these melons going?" asked Ian.

"To dah fah-mah's mah-kit in Jackson. Peoples who ain't got no gah-din goes deah tah git 'em a melon." Quincy reached in his back pocket and pulled out a pack of Garrett snuff. "Heah, try dis," he said as he reached his snuff out to Ian.

Ian put a pinch in his mouth. "This is the worst stuff I've ever tasted!" he proclaimed, as he spat the snuff on the ground.

Quincy smiled. "I ain't gone give you no mo'. I fo' sho' ain't gone waste no mo'. I kin tell ya' dat."

Ian was frustrated that he needed another bath so soon. Then something very striking occurred. Quincy had kept Ian so busy with the watermelons that he had not had the opportunity to notice until that moment. Two rows over, several small children were busy picking melons. They also knew the tricks to picking ripe melons.

"Hey, Quincy," said Ian.

"Yep?"

"Are those children only out here because of the break in elementary school?"

"Hmmph. Most o' 'em be Lena's gran chillen's. Dey be out in dah fiels till all dah cott'n crop come in, which ain't fo' nuthah munth o' so."

One of the children was fair-skinned, which caught Ian's attention. "Quincy, why is she so light-skinned compared to the rest of the children?"

"Hmmph," Quincy grumbled again. "You don't knows, do ya'? She be whut dey call a moo-lah-tah."

"What is a mulatto?" Ian asked, as he surmised the correct pronunciation.

"List'n, I know you be a greenho'n, but you may not believe dis. Huh mama be black, but huh daddy be white. Dat's whut a mulatto is, one black pah-ent an' one white pah-ent."

"My goodness. I've never heard of a mulatto."

"Hmmph, I kin tell. Deah be quite a few o' 'em 'roun' heah."

"Do you know the parents?"

"Sho' do." Ian took Quincy's curt answer to mean he didn't want to name the parents. It was time to change the subject.

"How long do they go to school?"

"Use'lly 'bout fo' tah fi' months. Us'lly, 'roun' Tanksgivin' tah Ma-ah-ch. Dat be dah onliess' time whin dey ain't needed in dah fiels."

As Ian stood in the back of the truck, two of Lena's grandchildren stepped into plain view. They had been too busy to notice the white man. None of the children wore shoes. Rather, their feet were wrapped in rags.

Rather naively, Ian remarked, "Quincy, Look! They aren't wearing any shoes! I guess that is a trick that they use to help you in the fields, huh Quincy? What, does it make their feet cooler in this humidity?"

"Hmmph, dat ain't dah reasun. Dey ain't got no shoes. Rags be all dey got."

Ian thought he had seen it all. But this was, by far, the most appalling thing that he had ever witnessed. As the children kept about their business, Ian was dumbfounded. He had never heard the white man's excuse for treating blacks as their slaves. The Southern preachers claimed that they could justify it from the Bible, because Ham, one of Noah's three sons, and one of eight who survived the Flood, was cursed for looking at his naked father. They preached that Noah himself said his son would be a servant to his two brothers, Shem and Japheth. Southern ministers adamantly alleged that that was why the Hamites were black--because they were cursed to be servants.

"Got moon pies in dah truck. It be 'bout dinnah time. Want one?"

"Yes, please." But Ian could not take his eyes off of the children's blistered feet. Ian bit into the banana moon pie. After seeing the plight of these black Delta children, he could not finish his snack.

"Thought you be hongry," Quincy sad.

"Not any more."

Quincy noticed that Ian was very moved by what he saw and remarked, "Dat jest dah way it be. Dat jest dah way it be."

The two men were through picking watermelons for the day. "Ah-ite, you ready fo' sum ho'in'?"

"Hoeing?" asked Ian, as if he didn't understand.

"Yep. Whin you's gittin' all cleaned up inside dat manshun, I wint ovah an' checked out dah cott'n. Rows need thinnin' out sum. Come on, I shows yah." Quincy went by the shed and picked up two hoes. "Dis cotton got a good stand. Dis gone be dah second time dis summah it bin hoed. You only wants cott'n plants evuh foot o' so. Enythang in between gotsta' cum out wid dah hoe. Can't hab no grass o' weeds in deah. If'n you don't thin it out, it staht robbin' dah cotton plant o' sunshine. Make sense, don't it?"

After two hours of hoeing with Quincy, Ian developed blisters in the palms of his hands. Quincy observed Ian clutching his hands. Ian was mulling over what to do when he saw Quincy looking at him. "Oh yeah, I only show you how tah git dah crick outta' neck, din't I? I fo'gots all 'bout yo' blistahs frum wuckin' wid Bessie Lee."

"Don't tell me; you have a remedy for my hands, too, right?"

"Yep. We take cah o' 'em tah-night at dah house."

An hour before sunset, the men stopped hoeing. Ian's hands hurt so badly that he could barely hold the hoe's handle. He and Quincy soon returned to the mansion.

"Yo' hands wouldn't hab blistahs if'n you do dis evuh day fo' a week o' two," Quincy said.

Mrs. Morganson was sitting in her favorite rocking chair on the back porch, drinking lemonade. "Quincy, I know this is the summer time, and we usually don't kill any hawgs till December, but we got one who seems to be 'bout ready to kill ovah. Ask Lester; he'll show you. You kin kill it and dress it if you want to. Like always, you kin have the head, feet, and the intestines."

Ian felt ready to gag. Intestines? Head? Feet? She *must* be kidding, he mused.

"Yass'um. You ra-at, I take it an' kill dat hawg. I be glad tah git dah head an' feet' an' insides. Make good chittlins an' souse." Quincy left to find Lester while Ian remained by the back porch.

"Come on up heah," ordered Mrs. Morganson. "Have a seat. Lena!"

"Yass'um," Lena responded through the back screen door.

"Git Mr. Smythe a tall glass o' ice lemonade. Have a seat, Mr. Smythe. You can call me Jean if you would like. My husband isn't here t'day. He's gone on business. But he'll back this afternoon. Will you be heah to meet him?"

"I doubt it." Ian had not forgotten what a travesty he had witnessed while the children toiled in the watermelon patch. As far as he was concerned, the sooner they got away from there, the better. "Mrs. Morg-,"

Mrs. Morganson held out her hand to touch Ian's. "Please, Jean will do."

"Oh, thank you. I noticed some children out there in the watermelon garden. They..."

Ian was interrupted again, this time by a beautiful young lady exiting the back door. Ian guessed that she was eighteen or nineteen years old. She was wearing a yellow-and-white striped cotton dress with full skirt and clear glass buttons. To Ian's surprise, the young lady was barefoot.

"Oh, Louise, meet Mr. Ian Smythe."

"Hello," said Louise.

Ian stood to greet the Morganson's only heir.

"Please, just call me Ian."

"Your accent is different from ours. Weah you from?"

There was a momentary pause before he answered Louise. Ian gulped down the remainder of his lemonade as he thought about Louise's statement, especially when he detected a strong Southern drawl from her lips. "Cambridge, England. I'm here to the black blues musicians of the Delta."

"Oh, my! Can't say that I evuh huhd of anybody comin' to these pahts to do such. Have you, Mama?"

"No," answered Mrs. Morganson, all the while staring at Ian. "Can't say that I have."

"I have heard I may not be the first to visit from England; but I do believe I am the first to stay this long. Also, I doubt my fellow Englishmen worked in the fields when they visited."

Ian was quickly attracted to Louise. He hoped that she would be interested in seeing him again.

Quincy trudged up, carrying a small flour sack. Ian sensed that Quincy was ready to leave.

"How long will ya' be stayin' in these parts?" asked Louise.

"I'm afraid I don't know exactly. One day, I will have to return home to England."

Quincy nodded to the pair of women. "See ya' latuh' Lena. I's gonna' need a new quilt dis wintah. I hopes you kin make me one. One I got's wo' out. Dun' said good bye to Dovie Ruth."

Lena smiled and added, "Ah-ite, I wuck on a quilt latuh in dah fall. Aftuh dah cott'n be pickt."

"Maybe we'll see ya' ah-gin, Mr. Smythe," Mrs. Morganson said.

"Miss Mo'gensen, whin I gots a 'roun' tah weah Lesta' wuz, he almose finished dressin' dat hawg," said Quincy. "I sho' do thank ya' fo' dah pickin's do'."

"Oh, you're quite welcome. One more thang, Quincy. Heah," said Mrs. Morganson, as she held out her hand.

Ian couldn't tell what it was that Mrs. Morganson handed Quincy. It appeared to be small sheets of paper, the size of a small notepad. Quincy and Ian walked to the car. Quincy set the flour sack on the back floorboard. The two men got into the car and left. Everything was vastly different in the Delta farmland from Cambridge, England. But, there was one thing Ian knew he would enjoy very much. That was, of course, getting to see Louise Morganson again.

"I seed ya' eyeballin' huh," said Quincy.

"I won't deny that. She is quite lovely."

"Yep; well jest remembuh, she be thuh mastuh's daughtah. Dat's all I gotsta' say."

Fourteen

IAN STUCK HIS HEAD out the window while he drove. Quincy had to ask. "Whut you be doin' *now*?"

"I need to get some fresh air with this sweaty shirt I am wearing. I already need another bath."

"Hmmph. Ma-at as well git useta' it. Be lack dat all dah time." Riding down Highway 1, Quincy continued, "You lucky. In all dah yeahs I bin 'roun' dat plantation, I ain't nevuh bin inside dah Mo'gensen's mane-shun."

"You are joking."

"No I ain't. Most o' us black labo-uhs git anyweah frum dollah en a haf tah two dollahs a day wuckin' fo' dah Mo'gensen's. Deah bin meny days way back wuckin' fo' Junyah's daddy weah we went tah sleep hongry. Eb'n whin we *did* hab sumpin' tah et, it might not be nuttin' but greens an' flow-ah gravy, maybe sum bread o' onions an' cone meal. You din't heah Miss Mo'gensen offah eny a dat lem'nade tah Lena o' me, did you? Cose not! An' she wadn't *fixin'* tah. I ain't tryin' tah soun' bittah. Dat's jest dah way it be."

Ian shook his head in disbelief. He smelled a foul odor, which, he assumed, was coming from his shirt. "I really do smell, don't I?"

"You ain't dah only thang you be smellin'." Quincy reached over the seat and grabbed the flour sack. "Dese pickin's, dat whut you be smellin', too."

"Pickings?" Ian asked.

"Yep. You know, dah hawg's leftovahs."

"Well, since I have my head out the window, anyway, I may as well throw up."

Quincy shook his head in bewilderment. "Did you see Miss Mo'gensen gib me sum papuh's whin we fixin' to leab?"

"Yes. What *were* those?"

"Dat was ow-ah payment fo' pickin' melons. She gib it tah me in scrip. See?"

"What is scrip?" Ian asked, as he took one of the papers.

"Scrip be sumpin' lack stamps, I reckon' you could say. I kin git stuff at dah sto' wid it. It kinda' lack money, 'ceptin' it ain't real money."

Ian gave Quincy a look like he didn't understand. "Hey, Quincy, have you ever driven a vehicle?"

"Me? Now, whin do you thank I woulda' got'n tah drive a cah? Ain't nevuh had one."

Ian pulled over onto a dirt road. "It's time you got a chance." Quincy froze at first. Then he looked toward Ian and grinned. "Ah-ite."

"For a change, I get to show *you* how to do something! Just be ready to put on the brakes in case something or someone pulls out in front of us."

"Ah-ite," Quincy said smiling.

"Just put your foot on the accelerator, and don't forget: be ready to use that brake." Quincy drove the jet-black 1954 Chrysler New Yorker for the next two miles. "You are driving very well for your first time."

"Ah-ite, did 'nuff. You bes' git back ovah heah b'fo' sumpin' happin." The two men exchanged seats. "Dat wadn't dat hahd aftuh all. By dah way, whose cah is dis? I knows you din't bring it all dah way frum Englan'."

"You are correct," Ian replied, smiling. "I know this will sound hard to believe; but, when I was in a Memphis pub—I mean, a Memphis juke joint, I met a man desperate for cash. He rented it to me, even though I had no Tennessee driver's license. I think he had had too much to drink. I gave him fifty dollars. He just said to be careful, for it has a four-barrel carburetor and two hundred and thirty-five horsepower. I have his address to return the car later."

Quincy then suggested that they visit Luthah Ray to learn about quill-making. Ian had two reasons he could be thankful for Quincy's suggestion. The more obvious reason was that he was going to learn how to make quills. The second reason was that he would get some needed rest. While driving to Luther Ray's, Ian kept thinking about Lena's grandchildren and the mulatto child. An hour before dusk, the men reached Luther Ray's.

"I sees 'eem out back, messin' wid Bessie Lee."

"Hey deah, boys! Look heah, Quincy. Bessie Lee dun got dah scabs," Luther Ray said.

"Yep, sho' do'," Quincy agreed, as he observed Bessie Lee's thick neck.

"Look heah, Ian. See dem scabs she got? It be frum weahin' dah collah. I shoulda' cleaned huh collah dah uthah day."

Quincy nodded as he offered a Lucky Strike to Luther Ray, who accepted it. "Got sumpin' else fo' ya." Holding out the sack, Quincy continued. "Miss Mo'gensen fin'ly had Lestah kill dat ol' hawg. Dis heah's dah pickin's. I'd lack tah keep dah feet fo' myself, do'. Also, I showed Ian how tah fish. Takes 'eem down tah my fa-vuh-ite spot. I'm almose' outta' ice. You kin hab 'em. Dat way, you kin cook 'em an' invite me ovah fo' a fish fry soon," Quincy added, with a smile.

"Ah-ite, ah-ite, thank ya." Luther Ray, though grateful for Quincy's gift, never looked inside the bag before setting it down. Ian would discover later why Quincy requested the pig's feet.

"Dis oughta' do it," Luther Ray said as he rubbed Bessie Lee's sore.

"What is that stuff?" asked Ian.

"Jimsonweed. Dat's 'nuthuh rem-uh-dee o' ow-ah's. Sumtimes we bawl peach leaves an' puts dem on deah. Dat wuck, too. 'N fac, whin we gots dah fevah ouhselves, we takes a bath in peach leaves. It wuck, too!"

Quincy nodded in agreement while Luther Ray whispered something in Bessie Lee's left ear. "I tell huh it gone be ah-ite. You see, a mule got twice as much sense as a hoss do."

"Luther Ray," Ian said, "I noticed you don't have a creek anywhere nearby. All I see is cotton. So, where do you get *your* water?"

"Cum heah. I show ya'. You see up deah? Whin dah rain hit dah roof, it gots tah cum down. Well, den it run off in dis heah trough. Den, aftuh it go intah dah trough, it go down intah dis sis-tuhn. See heah? Den, I takes a bucket wid a rope on it, an' draw it outta' bottom o' dah sis-tuhn. It ain't hahd. But, whin I needs tah take a bath, I jest tuhn ovuh dis tub an' catch sum rain wah-tuh."

"Hey, Luther Ray, let's you an' me shows Ian how tah make quills."

"Oh, ah-ite, sho' thang."

The trio walked over to a makeshift lean-to made from scrap lumber that was affixed to the house's north side. The roof was composed of indented corrugated tin, dotted with holes. Under this rough shed lay a stack of bamboo Luther Ray had cut earlier from the swamp near Quincy's place. "Fust o' all, you gots tah have 'bout six o' eight diffn't sizes o' cane. You don't want nun ob 'em dah same size. Den you ties 'em togetuh wid a piece o' dah fi-buhr, lack dis. But you still ain't ready tah staht playin' it. Next, you gotta' put two mo' pieces on dah back side. One go straight across, an' dah uhthah one go caddy cone-ah. Lack dis."

Ian was fascinated at how quickly the panpipe was made.

"Heah, try it," Luther Ray said, holding it out for Ian.

Ian began to blow on his new musical instrument. "I like it! Now, if I can just learn how to play it."

"You ain't gone fine' no music book on dah quill," Quincy said. "You jest gotsta' luhn lack all o' us. Dat's all."

Sitting on Luther Ray's porch, all three began to play. Soon Ian recognized what a novice he was at the panpipes--which was why he listened as much as he played. He would join in with Quincy and Luther Ray only when he felt confident. However, the two blues men seemed to be enjoying the time as much as Ian. After an hour or so, Quincy suggested it was time for them to leave, and they said their goodbyes to Luther Ray.

Fifteen

September--Cotton Season

    IAN WAS SLEEPING SOUNDLY that morning at four o' clock when he felt a nudge against his knee. "Time tah git up."
    Ian had now lived with Quincy for almost five weeks. He had learned many things from his mentor; but, he had learned from others as well. Happy Jefferson, Luther Ray, Lena Stokes, Dovie Ruth, and Quartez had taught Ian in one month more than he could have ever imagined. Furthermore, it was becoming clearer to Ian what Quincy meant when he said: "You gotsta' have dah blues tah play dah blues." There really *was* logic in what Quincy and others had been saying. One must *have* the blues to play them to the best of their ability! Ian was not going to learn as much about playing the blues until he had experienced what the Southern black man had.
    The invaluable porch lessons with the fife, guitar, harmonica, fiddle, and quills had made Ian realize that he was a long way from where he wanted to be in his blues playing. Yet, he also felt that he had matured in his playing and made progress in his understanding of the black man's plight.
    "Cott'n time. Let's go see Mistah Mo'gensen."
    Although Ian was very tired, he was glad to hear Quincy's news. Ever since his initial drive from Memphis, Ian had been seeing that white stuff in the fields. He had picked melons near it, and on two occasions, he had thinned out weeds around it. Now, the time had finally come. He would get to experience picking the king crop of the South. Furthermore, he thought to himself, he would get to see Louise again.
    Quincy and Ian ate the usual breakfast of biscuits and molasses. They then walked to the car using the flashlight. "Oh yes, I've been meaning to ask: why is it that my fingers seem to clam together?" asked Ian.
    "Hmmph, dat be dah hoo-mid-ah-tee. It make ya' real sticky. It **always** be heah. But I knowd some peoples who visited Cal-ah-fo'-nya yeahs 'go who say deah ain't no hoo-mid-ah-tee deah. It too dry. Hmmph, I sho' would lack tah feel whut dat be lack."
    "Isn't it a bit early to be leaving?"
    "No. Lack I dun tole you once, we pick from Can't See tah Can't See. Dat mean we pick from b'fo' sunup tah aftuh sundown."

Enroute to the Morganson Plantation, as John Lee Hooker's *Dimples* aired on the radio, Ian wondered if he had the stamina to last from Can't see to Can't see. Quincy smoked three cigarettes back to back. Ian and Quincy were beginning to know each other rather well. They had been together each waking moment for the last five weeks. Occasionally, they could guess what the other was thinking. However, the most cherished asset of all to Ian was the two men's developing friendship. Certainly, Ian had found his mentor. And Quincy discovered something that many of his black neighbors and fellow laborers had not. He had found that not every white man was bigoted, and that some really *could* be trusted. The Southern black man had been just as guilty of stereotyping the white man as the white man had with the black man.

The two men drove down the Morganson driveway as they had done several times before. Quincy directed Ian to drive around the big house, onto a narrow lane that cut off of the main driveway. Quincy instructed Ian where to park. As always, Ian glanced over to the back porch. He knew Louise would not be there at that time of morning, but he had to look, anyway.

Soon it was light enough to see. Quincy thumped out his fourth cigarette of the morning and informed Ian it was almost time to start picking. Several other black laborers were gradually making their way to Quincy's vicinity. Although Ian never heard it said, it was obvious to Ian that Quincy was a quiet leader of the black workforce. "Hopefully," Quincy commented, "by dah en' o' dah day, you kin say you pickt two hun-ded fifty pound."

Ian definitely wanted to please Quincy in whatever he did. He kept reminding himself that this experience would benefit him in the long run. Ian thought equally as much of Louise Morganson. Maybe he would see her today. Soon the men were in the field, picking the white stuff. There were no breaks other than twenty minutes for lunch, which consisted of two moon pies and an RC Cola. The Delta humidity offered no breezes, nor so much as a small breath. Ian was learning the hard way that the Mississippi Delta took its toll on all men, black and white.

Ian dragged his last croaker sack of the day to the tractor trailer, where Quincy weighed it. "Two hunded an' fifty-fo' pound! You did it!" Ian was dead tired; but he hadn't felt so good in a long, long time. Now, if he only could find the energy to drive them home. On the way to the car, Ian could not resist looking toward the mansion's back porch. That was where a maiden usually sat to pass the day away. There was not much else for a Southern belle to do on a Mississippi Delta plantation, isolated from the rest of the planet. To Ian's delight, Louise *was* sitting in the swing, flipping through the pages of the latest Montgomery Ward catalogue. Unbeknownst to Ian, Louise had been watching him out of the corner of her eye.

"Hello, Louise, remember me?"

"Oh yes, of course I do," Louise said, pretending as though she was surprised at his presence.

Ian knew this would not be good timing for a long conversation, for one of Louise's parents was always in the house. But at least he got to see her. *At least*, she remembered him. One day, he would get to speak at length with Louise--unless he had to return to England.

Mr. Leonard Morganson came to the door. "Daddy, have you met Ian?" asked Louise.

"Nawh, I ain't. Glad to meet ya'. I'm Leonard Morganson. You prob'ly huhd by now that mos' of 'em 'roun' heah jest call me 'Junyah'."

"Yes, hello. I have heard them call you Junior."

"Well, I must go, Honey chile'. Got tah go see Mr. Wakefield in Drew. Nice to meet ya', Ian."

"Likewise."

That was the extent of Ian's conversations with Mr. Morganson; always brief but cordial. Junior was a busy man and was always on the go, leaving almost everything at the plantation in the hands of his foreman, Charlie Short. Charlie didn't talk except when necessary. The blacks had always felt Charlie treated them fairly, much more fairly than the levee camp bosses of decades past. In fact, they preferred dealing with Charlie in lieu of Junior any day.

The men returned to the levee house. As usual, Quincy pulled out his guitar, harmonica, fife, and quills. And as usual, Ian was dead tired and content to merely listen. As far as he was concerned, it was the sweetest, most supreme music anyone had ever played. Ian began to realize that playing was Quincy's way of dealing with the hardships he had to endure. Some people deal with their grief and anger by lashing out. The wealthy see psychiatrists, while the indigent may be cast away in an asylum, too poor and uneducated to defend themselves. Not Quincy, however; he returned to his porch chair each night. That was Quincy Quarles' therapy, playing and singing.

The rain began to fall as the men retired for the night.

"What's that noise?" Ian asked.

Quincy set an old lard bucket under a ceiling leak. "Jest 'nuthah leak. Gotsta' fix dat one o' dese days. Soon, I shows you how us black folk make tea." But Ian made no reply. Quincy then remembered it was Ian's first day at picking cotton. Peeping over at Ian's cot, Quincy saw that he was sleeping soundly. Soon, thought Quincy, soon, he would show Ian how to make sassafras tea.

FOUR O' CLOCK A.M. came quickly. "Time tah go back tah dah fiels."

Ian dragged himself out of bed. The consolation was that he would get to hear the blacks sing some of their field hollerings. He was amazed at the group's harmony and rhythm. They had never had a music teacher, nor did they have the words written down; they were mostly illiterate, anyway. Yet, as far as Ian was concerned, they were far greater than the largest Anglican choir in all of England.

Every day on the Morganson Plantation, Ian's thoughts turned more and more to Louise. He was unsure of how she may feel toward him. Once, while picking melons behind the mansion, he looked at an upstairs window and thought he saw someone looking in his direction. He couldn't be certain; but it looked like Louise. An occasional hello or goodbye only frustrated him, for it only made him want to know more about her. The blues Quincy sang at night on the porch seemed appropriate to express Ian's feelings, too. One day he would have to go back to Cambridge. He must make his move soon if he was going to find out if she cared anything about him. Ian's break came on a Thursday. The cotton pickers retired early. Louise and one of her best friends were on the back porch.

"Ian, I want you to meet my friend, Freddie Lou Slater," said Louise.

"Hello. Pleased to meet you, Freddie Lou."

Quincy interrupted, "You 'bout ready tah go? I needs tah stop at dah sto'. I's be outta' smokes." The two men made their way to Ian's car. "Freddie Lou's whut we calls a tomboy 'roun' heah."

After the men were out of earshot, Freddie Lou commented to Louise, "You're right; he *is* cute. Say he's from England, huh?"

"Yes, and one day, he will have to go back."

Freddie Lou detected a solemn tone in Louise's voice. "Can't for the life of me figure why such a nice-looking white boy would volunteer to git out in the fields with the black folk to pick cott'n an' melons an' sech. Jest don't make sense to me."

Louise offered no reply to Freddie Lou, preferring to watch the two men headed toward the car.

Once he was near the car, Quincy bent down and grabbed something between two fingers. He had spotted one of cotton's main nemeses, the boll weevil. Quincy called it *"Anthonomus Grandis,"* as he let it scamper freely in his palm.

"I beg your pardon?"

"Dis heah, *Anthonomus Grandis.* Dat be dah boll weevil's real name. County ag man tole me dat once. Miss Pah-kuh down at dah sto' useta' pay us a penny apiece fo' dese whin we'd bring 'em in. Mistah Pah-kuh pours coal oil on 'em tah kills 'em. Dat's befo' cottn' pois'n came pop'luhr."

BILLIE MAE was in the back of the store when Quincy and Ian arrived. Ian looked around for some chips and candy to purchase. For years, Quincy had wanted to use an indoor facility, but he had never been asked inside at the Morganson's. None of Quincy's friends had ever had indoor plumbing, either.

"Whut dat say on dat do'?"

"Oh, it says, 'Customer's Restroom. Whites On—'." Quincy knew what Ian was about to say.

"I bin wantin' tah use one o' dem fo' yeahs."

"Go ahead." He did not tell Quincy that he was keeping a lookout for Mrs. Billie Mae. After a few minutes, a nervous Ian asked, "You okay in there, Quincy?"

Quincy did not respond; Ian stuck his head in the door. Quincy was on his knees, washing his hands in the toilet.

"What are you doing?"

"I's be washin' my hans'. What'd you thank I be doin'?"

"That's not where you wash your hands."

"Ain't? What it be fo' din?"

Ian looked back toward the counter. Mrs. Billie Mae was returning from the back door.

"Quick, come on! I'll tell you later."

The two men scurried to the potato chip rack before Mrs. Billie Mae saw them. Ian thought to himself that if Quincy ever joked to others about Ian's being a greenhorn, then Ian was definitely going to inform them about Quincy's washing his hands in the toilet of a public restroom.

IAN NOTICED a few new faces among the black laborers at the plantation the next morning. It seemed to Ian the new cotton pickers were assembled as clans. "Quincy, why are they here?"

"Dey be's heah fo' dah scrappin's. You 'el be seein' latuh."

When Quincy and Ian retired for the day, the families trudged out to the same rows where Quincy and Ian had already picked. They were carrying flour sacks, and Ian watched out of curiosity. The families—father, mother, and children—cleaned the plants completely bare. For a brief moment, Quincy felt as though he really was Ian's mentor. "See, dat why I tole you fust day tah not wuh-ee 'bout gittin' eb'ry single piece o' cottn' off dah plant. I knew dis day was a cummin'."

"What do they do with such *little* cotton?"

"Dey cleans dah plant real good an' take what's dey git tah dah gin. Dey sells it fo' food. It kina' lack leftovahs, I reckon' you could say."

Ian was exhausted from the day's picking. But his heart went out to the families just as it did the first time he saw the little boys and girls whose feet were wrapped in rags. John Lee Hooker's *No Shoes* came to mind.

No food on my table,
And no shoes to go on my feet,

*No food on my table,
And no shoes to go on my feet.*

*My children cry for mercy,
They ain't got no place to call their own.
Hard times, Hard times,
They seem like they's here to stay
If somebody don't help me...
Children cryin' fo' bread.*

Ian had begun to feel a gradual looseness in the work clothes he wore. Weighing himself on one of the cotton scales, Ian discovered that, in five weeks of living with Quincy, he had lost twenty-two pounds. The thought then occurred to him that he had never seen a fat black child. Now he knew why.

The night went quickly. Quincy woke Ian at five o' clock the next morning.

"Time tah git up."

"Huh?"

With eyes barely opened, Ian saw Quincy starting a fire. Quincy pushed the ashes to the back of the wood stove. Then he put something in front of the ashes.

"Huh? We *ain't* got no cott'n to pick." Ian noticed that his vernacular was changing. For the first time in his life, Ian spoke in slang. Even Quincy noticed it, giving Ian a quick stare.

"Hmmph, maybe so. But we's fixin' tah go huntin'. You still don't want no coffee?"

"No, thank you. I sure would like a cup of hot tea, though."

Quincy heard Ian, but made no comment. A few moments later, the two men entered the woods.

"Ain't dah same no mo'."

"What isn't the same any more?"

"No Slick wid me. He wuz a' good hep." Ian was instructed by his mentor to watch where he walked. Stepping on crunchy leaves let the critters know someone was coming, giving them ample time to flee. A few more minutes passed before Quincy spotted a gray squirrel scurrying on the limb of a scrubby pine. Quincy squeezed the trigger on his shotgun, and the squirrel fell. "Now I gotsta' fetch 'em myself. Use tah, I coul dee-pen on Slick fo' dat. Ca-eh tah try tah shoot dis thang?" Silently, slowly, Ian took the gun. "Theah be at least two thangs you need tah know 'bout shootin' dis heah twelve gauge. One, don't put yo' fingah on dah triggah till you be ready tah shoot. It be danj-uh-us; plus, can't affode tah waste no shells. Deah's an ah-mah-dil-lah cummin'."

"How do you know? Do you see it?"

"Nawh, not yet. But heah how it be draggin' 'roun'? It make a lotta' noise cummin' through dah woods. Dey must be almose blind an' deaf 'cuz us'lly you kin get real close tah 'em befo' dey evah sees ya'. Din, if'n he *do* see ya', he be jumpin'--straight up." After a brief pause, Quincy spotted the armadillo. "See, deah he be. Aim an' pulls dah triggah whin you know it ra-at dead on 'eem."

Ian did exactly as Quincy showed him. He fired the gun, but he was not prepared for such a kickback. He almost fell back off his feet. "Why didn't you tell me that it would kick me like that?"

"I'z fixin' tah. Dat was dah secon' thang you needed tah know befo' you shoots at anythang. Look lack you gots 'eem, do'. Let's go see."

About sixty feet away lay the armadillo, lying on its side. Ian didn't know whether to feel sorry for killing an animal or to feel glad because he was getting more skilled at what the Delta black man did to survive.

"Ah-mah-dil-lah gots ah skin lack nuttin' else I knows. He be real tough. Twelve-gauge, do', he can't suh-vive dat."

The two men began walking back to the house, carrying one gray squirrel and one heavy, imbricated armadillo. Ian wondered if he could stomach the two animals at the dinner table.

"Ho' up. You be wantin' tea, huh?"

Ian nodded, but he was very suspicious of Quincy's ability to obtain tea, especially out in the middle of a patch of woods.

"Well din, we fixin' tah see whud we kin do 'bout dat. Dis heah tree--see dah roots on it? Dat sasparilla roots."

Ian quickly corrected Quincy. "Don't you mean *sar*saparilla roots?"

"No. Dat's why I brung dis heah spade. We gone dig up sum roots. Taste ra-at good whin ya' add sugah o' milk tah it." Kneeling down, Quincy showed Ian how to dig up the tree's roots. Then he placed them in the bag of game. After returning to the house, Quincy advised Ian how to clean the squirrel and armadillo. "Wid out Slick heah, look lack I don't need tah keep dah 'testin's,'" Quincy said, making conversation. "Less'n, cose, *you* wants 'em." Ian, however, shuddered at the thought.

Later, in the house, Quincy handed Ian a Mason jar. "Heah, try dis." Ian had learned it did little good to protest. Quincy would always say, "Okay, din, you gone go back on yo' wuhd."

Ian drank the jar's contents. "What was that?" Ian asked.

"Re-mem-buh I aks Luther Ray if'n I could keep dah pigs' feet? Well, I be grindin' 'em up in dah stove. Dey crumble up reals good aftuh dey bin in dah fi-ah good while. Almost lack bread. Den you put 'em in wah-tuh an' boil 'em. Dat be what you dun drank—hog hoof." Quincy smiled as he carefully watched Ian's reaction. Ian did not know whether to go outside and disgorge his drink or just tolerate it as best as he could.

"Deah still be lots fo' yah tah luhn befo' you gotsta' r'tuhn tah England. I ain't nevuh eb'n showed yah how tah clean lahd."

"Lahd?" What's lahd?"

"It be dah fat off o' dah hawg. Sumtimes I makes crackles outta' it. Some peoples call 'em cracklin's, but I's call 'em crackles. Dey be *sum kinda'* good. I us'lly puts a drop o' soda an' salt in it. Dat make it white. Ain't gon' shows you how tah smoke meat, 'cause I ain't got no smoke house down heah at dis house. Dun it yeahs ago, do'. Ain't showed you enythang 'bout hog head sausage, neithuh. 'Roun' heah, we calls it souse."

"Souse?"

"Yep, you may o' huhd it call pickled pig feet. Didn't git tah shows you how tah pick buttah beans, hows tah shell 'em, hows tah put 'em up, hows tah preserve, hows tah dig up tatuhs, how tah can vejt'bls, jam, jelly, how tah make a drum fo' playin' outta' a fifty-pound lahd ba-el, or how tah make lye soap, homemade ice cream or sassafras o' pine top tea whilst dah sap's down. Lawd, dah longah I sits heah, dah longah I thinks o' thangs you still could luhn, lack raisin' yahdbuhds an' goats, hows tah roll ya' own cee-gahs wid molasses on it tah makes it stick togath--."

"Yes, yes, I get the idea."

"Oh, an' cone lickah, I nevuh gotsta' show you 'bout dat. You take Luthah Ray, now, he makes dah bess' cone lickah dese pahts. We's us'ly calls it white lightnin'. You take Dovie Ruth an' Lena, now, dey's kin shows yah how tah make quilts an' baskets an' stuff lack dat."

"The first Sunday I was in the Delta, I visited Happy's Mount Nebo Missionary Baptist Church. I have noticed that since I have been here, Quincy, *you* don't attend church," remarked Ian.

"Yeah, I knows jest weah Happy's ch-uch be." Quincy paused for a moment. "Naawh, you ra-at, deah be a reason why I ain't gone tah chh-uch since you bin heah. Simple, really. I be's protectin' yah."

"Huh?"

"Well, you tole me 'bout dat Dep-ah-tee Puhvis. Den dah Klan cum ovah heah dat night. Lookt lack dah bess' thang fo' us tah do wuz lay low. Dey mean bizness. You might git huht. So, I bin stickin' on you lack fuzz do a peach."

"You, too. You could have gotten hurt, too." Quincy nodded. "Fo' sho'."

Ian paused. "Have they ever hurt you, Quincy?"

"Who dat?"

"The KKK or any of the white men?"

"Hmmph." It was easy to tell he did not want to remember those days.

Ian felt something crawling on his neck. With the tip of his thumb and index finger, he was able to pinch it and pull it off. "What is this, Quincy?" he asked, as he held it in Quincy's view.

"Hmmh, dat be a tick. Millun's ob 'em 'roun' heah. Throw it down." Quincy quickly stepped on it, then added, "Dey stays on you too lone an' dey kin suck dah blood ra-at outta' yah. You got dat 'un early. Dey useta' bothuh Slick in summah time 'specially. Good thang we ain't run intah no chiggahs yet. Dey makek you itch as much as okra an' peach fuzz."

That night Quincy roasted peanuts, another product of the Morganson Plantation. Opening his wood stove, Quincy commented, "I calls 'em a delicacy. Sumtime, we boil 'em instaid." As they sat on the porch that night enjoying the peanuts, Quincy saw a car's headlights near Ian's car. Both men rose to their feet as the lights went out. Quincy immediately checked his gun to be certain two shells were in the barrels.

"Slick wud be bahkin' 'bout now. Wush I had sum buckshot."

"I wonder if it is those white-robed men again," Ian said quickly.

"Prob'ly, but can't tell jest yet."

Whoever was out there in the dark was not very secretive. That was what was so baffling to both men; it seemed to the two men that the visitor was *trying* to be heard.

"They's as loud as ah-mah-dil-la cummin' through dah woods."

"Ian! Quincy?"

Both men recognized the voice immediately.

"Louise?" yelled Ian in return.

"Yes! It's just me!"

"Might be a trick," said Quincy.

"Huh?"

"Sho'. Dey may be tryin' tah coax us out wid Louise, seein' hows ev'ybody knows you two gotta' thang fo' each uthah."

Ian ran off the porch to meet Louise. "What are you doing here?"

"I did not know when you were goin' back to England. I wanted to say bye before you left."

"How did you find us?"

"It wadn't hard. I asked Lena. I've been down this road before. Just not this far down it, though."

"But your parents; surely they will wonder where you are."

"Most of the time, I'd say you're right. Fact is, though, they took a trip to New Awlins' and won't be back until Friday. I'm getting' the age where they let me decide if I want to go with them on trips sech as that."

"Are you in that mansion all by yourself?"

"No, she ain't," Quincy intervened. He had caught up with the pair in his front yard. "Dovie Ruth stays in thuh back shed. You must o' tole huh sumpin' fo' her tah let you git outta' dah house."

"I did, Quincy. For years, Dovie Ruth's wanted a record player. I told her that if she kept quiet and didn't tell anybody that I borrowed Daddy's car, I would buy her one."

"Hmmph."

"Well, won't you come up to the house?"

"Oh, okay."

After a few minutes, Quincy went inside. But he was not ready to turn in; he still had reservations of Louise's motive. He also watched with his shotgun in his lap for movement in the distance. For the next two hours, Ian and Louise chatted on the front porch, while Quincy smoked Lucky Strikes back to back inside the house.

"When will you be returning to England?"

"In two days, I'm afraid. As much as I would like to stay longer, I can not. I must be getting back. I've not spoken to my parents or anyone in England since I've been here. However, I have written them."

"Where did you mail your letters from?"

"I asked Mrs. Parker if she would take care of them."

"Have they ever responded?"

"Yes, I have two letters from them. They know I am okay and will be returning not too terribly long from now."

"I'll be sad to see you go,"

"Thank you. I was just getting to know you. One thing I have wondered, Louise. Are you still in school?"

"No, if you mean high school. I graduated last year and plan to go to Delta State University this coming January. I was supposed to start in August, but I didn't get all of my registration papers in on time. The university's in Cleveland, not too far from here."

"Yes, I've heard of Cleveland. Are you a procrastinator?"

"Huh?"

"You said you didn't get all of your papers in on time for the August session. Do you put off things easily and let them go for another day?"

"Not usually. I intentionally didn't have my papers turned in on time. Mama told Daddy that she wondered how I could be so silly as to let that happen. But I did it on purpose."

"On purpose? I am afraid I don't understand."

"I was almost finished with my registration for August, and then you showed up on my back porch."

Louise didn't need to explain any further. Ian was a bit embarrassed. "Well, I must admit, each time I came to your house with Quincy, I first looked on the back porch to see if you were there."

Both Ian and Louise began to smile at one another. No further explanation was necessary.

"What will you do when you return to England?"

"Start up a band. It's been my lifelong dream to have a band, one in which I could make some of the decisions. I've been in a couple of bands where my decisions and suggestions mattered little. My piano playing wasn't used as much as I felt it could be. When I heard those blues players who visited England, I knew then what kind of music I wanted to play."

Louise said, "I have a radio at the house, and Mama and Daddy have a record player. I listen mostly to Elvis Presley, Jerry Lee Lewis, and a little of Ray Orbison. I bought a couple of Elvis' seventy-eight's not long ago in Cleveland. I like Chuck Berry's music, too; but I know that my folks would kill me if they found out I had spent their money on a black musician."

"Too bad. Chuck Berry is one of America's finest musicians."

"Well, I must be going. I don't want to worry Dovie Ruth any more than necessary."

"Come with me," said Ian.

"Huh?"

"Come with me to England."

"Why, how would…," Louise began to say.

"Listen, I have never had a steady girlfriend. But if you would come, I would take care of you."

"Take care of me? What do you mean?"

"I would marry you, if you would let me." Ian was as surprised at his words as Louise was. But he wasn't going to retract his words now. He had fantasized of their marriage, but he had not dreamed of asking her under the present circumstances.

"Why, I don't know what to say."

"I hope you do not think I am acting spontaneously, simply from emotions. Ever since I first saw you, I have wondered what may become of us."

Louise appeared surprised. But it was really a dream come true. For several years, Louise had known that she did not want to live out her entire life on the Morganson Plantation. Even if it meant she would not inherit the plantation one day, she didn't care. She desperately wanted to get out of the Mississippi Delta cotton land somehow. What better way was there for her to get out than to elope with a young man whom she cared about and who cared about her? Yet, it was too soon for Louise to let Ian know her deepest feelings. "I'll have to think about it, of course. All of this is so sudden, you know."

"Yes, but it's because I have to leave soon. I tell you what, rather than eloping, why don't I go back to England and you work it out somehow? You can write me every week or so and let me know."

"Okay. I will try my best, but you might as well know, Ian, my parents will *never* approve of it."

"No, I thought not. Wait a moment. Let me write down my address for you."

Ian ran to the porch to get a pencil and paper. He wrote down his Cambridge address, and Louise got in her car and left, possibly seeing Ian Smythe for the last time. Then Ian returned to his favorite sitting spot on the porch.

Quincy came out the door. "Hmmph. She wadn't up tah no tricks aftuh all," he thought to himself.

"What do you think of her?" Ian asked Quincy.

"Oh, she be ah-ite. If'n she ain't spoilt ah-ready, she ma-at make sumbody a good wife."

Sixteen

QUINCY AND IAN sat at Quincy's kitchen table the next morning.

"Last night, you never did finish telling me about church."

"No, cum tah thank of it, I didn't, did I." There was a slight pause before Quincy continued. "I wuz a jackleg preachuh in my youngah days, mosely 'roun' Midnight an' Hahd Cash—dey be in Humphrees County, in dat err-ee-uh. I din't preach e'vy Sun-dee 'cause I couln't read dah Bib'l no ways. Jest stand up an' say what'd I re-membuhd uthah preachuhs say whin I's youngah.

"But whin my wife an' son died, well, I couln't take it no mo'. Jest lack in dah New Tes-tah-mint, weah it says sumpin' 'bout dem Chris-chuns bein' puh-see-ku-tid. Bin whipt by white boss man a few times, but dat ain't nuttin' cumpa-ed tah me losin' *dem*. An' black folks need sumpin' sayed tah dem frum dah pulpit dat ain't lack dah blues. Yeah, we sang lacks dat sumtimes in chh-uch. But whut dey really need is sum hope. An' whin my wife an' son pas' 'way, well, I couln't gib dem dah hope dat dey needs tah heah. So dat mo' o' less ended my preachin'."

Quincy chuckled. "But deah ain't nuttin' wrong wid goin' tah chh-uch on Sun-dee an' heah dah preachah preach his suh-mun an' praise dah Lawd. 'N fac', I tries tah go ev'ry chance I git. I us'ly go down south o' Rosedale, toe-ud Dahomey."

Ian interjected, "I played the piano in my church a few years ago back in Cambridge. I quit, though, when the organist demanded that I swap with her, meaning, she play the piano and I play the organ. She even went to the bishop about it. I like the organ, but my specialty is the piano. So, rather than argue about it with her, I just quit. Besides, there were others in the church who could play the ivories and take my place."

"Hmmh, hmmh," Quincy mumbled, shaking his head as though he fully understood. Then he lit up one of his homemade cigars.

"Quincy, I am leaving the day after tomorrow. I gave my word that I would only stay for two months."

"Ah-ite."

LATE THE NEXT DAY, at dusk, Quincy suggested, "You ready tah go sumweah?"

"Sure! Where?"

"You see."

"Okay, but first, I need to visit the outhouse." While Ian visited the antiquated facilities in the back, Quincy carried his guitar to the car, placing it on the back floorboard, behind the passenger's front seat and out of Ian's sight. He stuffed his harmonica in his front pants pocket. Then he returned to the house.

Ian returned soon to the front. "I'm ready if you are, Quincy."

Traveling south on Highway 1, Quincy directed, "Tuhn left heah, on dis road. We gone go tah Moun' City." *Devil Got My Woman* was blaring out Ian's radio.

Driving into Mound City, Ian asked, "Now where? So far, all I see is a barrelhouse ahead." The sign near the road identified the juke joint as Harvey's Night Spot.

"Pull in deah."

Ian's mouth dropped open. "But I don't understand, Quincy, you said..."

"I know whut I said. Seein' how's you be leavin', I thought one mo' time be ah-ite. Dat ain't all. Dah last time we saw Quo-tez, he tole me dat Hahvey ben askin' 'bout me an' dat white boy stayin' wid me fo' a couple o' munths. He tole Quo-tez he want me tah git ovah heah an' play 'gin. I tole Quo-tez tah tell Hahvey I see 'bout it fo' tonight. But dat still ain't all."

"Oh? What else is new?"

"Hahvey got a pianah inside," Quincy said as he exited the front door and opened the back door, pulling out his six-string guitar off of the floor. "So, let's do it."

Quartez, Luther Ray, Henry Bigsby, and a few other black blues musicians Ian had met over the last two months were already inside.

"Ian, it wouldn' happin tah be yo' buhthday, would it?" asked Luther Ray.

"No. Why do you ask, Luther Ray?"

"Cuz it might as well be. Quincy planned dis fo' you. Kinda' lack a goin' 'way pahty."

"Tonight, it gone be a lit'l dif-ah-ent," Quincy said to Ian. "So fah, all you ben heahin' is me an' a few o' dah boys play. But I ain't sayed nuttin' 'bout one o' dah bes' singahs. She be heah tonight."

"*She?*"

"Dat's ra-at. Sum o' dah bes' blues singahs be wom'n. One o' dah bes' 'un's 'roun' dese pahts gone sing tonight. *I* thank she soun' a lit'l lack Etta James. An' *you* gone be on dah pianah. We gone chip in on sum o' ow-ah instrahmints, so don't wuh-ee, Ian."

Ian was flabbergasted. "But I can't, why I am not qualified to play the blues. You can't let me..."

"Hush up, you gone play wid us. Don't wuh-ee 'bout no qual-ah-fah-ca-shuns."

A large woman in a red dress came through the front door.

"He she cum now," Quincy said, with a nod in the direction of the front door.

It was Leona Stokes. "Wait a minute, I'm confused here. Leona, are *you* the singer for tonight?"

"Hey deah, Ian. Sho' am."

"But, you didn't tell me you could sing when I visited your place."

"No, I reckon it nevah did cum up in ow-ah convahsation."

"Amazing! Amazing!"

For the next two hours, Leona sang while Quincy, Quartez, Henry, and Luther Ray alternately played harmonica, guitar, fiddle, fife, and quills. As Ian played the piano, tune after tune, he kept telling himself that this had to be the most significant and most memorable night he had experienced in the Delta of Mississippi. But sadly, his journey was about to come to a close.

Neither Quincy nor Ian said a word on the way home that night, but it was for different reasons. Quincy never talked that much, anyway. But Ian remained silent because he was still absorbing what had just occurred. If only his friends in England could be there!

As usual, the men settled down on Quincy's porch upon returning. "You have helped me more than you will ever know. I haven't learned the blues as well as you, and I probably never will," Ian said. "I think there are two reasons for that. One, I am just not quite as gifted as you are, Quincy. And the other, well, I just haven't experienced the blues like you have. At first I thought these two months were going to kill me. But they have turned out to be the best experience for me."

Quincy nodded as though he agreed with what Ian said. He pulled out his Garrett snuff, took a pinch, and placed it gingerly in his mouth. "You gibbin' me too much credit. Don't forgit, dah Lawd blesst me wid whatevah I can do wid a guitah o' hah-mon-ee-kah o' eny uthah instrament. But I ain't gone say dat dah Lawd caused me to play in dem ba-ell-houses. I dun dat on my own. Dat's all."

Ian said, "I have one more request from you. I have asked Louise to eventually join me in England. Will *you* come to England as well?"

"You dun *what*? Boy, you kin fo'git dat! Huh ol' man ain't gone let huh go tah no Englun'! And, did I tell you, I ain't nevuh bin outta' Delta my whole life?"

"So?"

Seventeen

Cambridge, England--1973

"--AND SO I LEFT the Mississippi Delta and returned to Cambridge, Mr. Jensen," Ian said.

Roger had been jotting a few notes on his pad, but his recorder was on as well.

"But, Mr. Smythe, I guess you know what my next question is."

"What happened to Louise Morganson and, of course, Quincy Quarles? Right?"

"Yes, that is *precisely* what I was about to ask."

"I gave my word to Quincy that I would never tell."

"It's okay, Ian," the butler said. "You kin tell 'eem now." With a slight pause, he added, "I be Quincy Quarles."

Roger rose from his chair, staring directly toward Quincy. Roger had come to visit Ian Smythe merely because that was what Mick, his manager, had instructed. He really didn't care much for rock and roll. But as Ian related the story of the Delta and many of the details, Roger found himself mesmerized. "I, I don't know what to say."

"Ian kep his wuhd. You dah fust tah knows who's I am, dat is, outside dis house."

"I am sorry, Mr. Quarles, but what do you mean by 'wuhd and fust'?"

"Wuhd means word," Louise interjected, "and fust means first."

"You see, Mistah Jensen, when you fust entered dah house t'day, I tried tah speak lack a real English butlah might. Dat cuz I din't wants ya' tah detec' my axcent. At dat moment, I wadn't sho' I wanted you tah know who I be. But truthfully, I ain't loss my Southern axcent."

"I know how you feel," Ian said to Roger. "It took me a few weeks before I could understand what Quincy was saying, and yet, there are *still* times when he mumbles something none of us understand."

"I'm honored to meet you," Roger said, holding out his hand to shake with Quincy's. "My, this is quite a surprise." Facing the two ladies, Roger had to know. "And you, could you possibly be Louise?"

Louise nodded. "I'm 'fraid so," she said with a slight smile.

Roger then asked the younger lady, "And you?"

"Me? Why, I'm their daughter," she replied.

Louise sensed further explanation was needed. "You see, Mr. Jensen, my name is Louise 'cause I was born in the Louise community, on the side of the road. Mama had me in the back seat of Daddy's car. Wadn't nobody in the car 'cept me, Mama, Daddy, and Lena. Mama wadn't 'xpectin' me for 'nother month and a half. But I came early. So, Mama told Daddy to pull over. Lena helped bring me into this world, seeing as how she was the midwife for so many folks back in those days."

"And Midnight," Ian added. "Guess where the band gets its name."

"I suppose there is a Midnight community in Mississippi?"

"Yep," replied Quincy. "It be neah dah Louise co-moon-ty. Fust time Ian heah me men-shun dat name, he decided tah name his next ban' by dat name. But he almose name it Hahd Cash, 'nuthah neahby co-moon-ty."

"Bet you can't guess my name," their daughter said.

"Dovie Ruth or Lena?"

"My name is Rose."

"That's right," Ian added. "The name Rose was taken from Rosedale. We had already decided that if Louise had a boy instead, we would name him Dale."

"But how did your parents react to your moving to England?" Roger asked Louise, as he continued to make an occasional paper notation.

"They didn't like it one bit," Louise replied. There was a long pause.

Ian intervened when he sensed Louise could not continue. "But, right after Louise informed her parents of her wishes, they were killed in a head-on car collision near Vicksburg. After writing me of what had occurred, I still offered Louise the opportunity to come. We were married the second week she was here. Rose was born about one year later. The rest is history."

"But what about the Morganson Plantation? Did you not stand to inherit all of that?"

"Yes," replied Louise, "and I *did* inherit all four thousand akuhs an' thuh big house and their bank holdin's. When I moved here, I still owned it. But I don't own it any more, Mr. Jensen. When Ian began to make lots of money on the rock and roll scene, he and I decided that we didn't need that place any more. Daddy didn't always treat the nig-- blacks as well as he should. After they died, I wanted no part of it. Kinda' like a stigma, you know?"

"So you sold it?"

"Yes. I sold it to a man who already owned one plantation."

Ian stood there, with his right elbow leaning on the fireplace mantel. Occasionally, he dragged on an extra-long cigarette. "I am sure you observed some of the farm implements coming down the driveway. Did you see the old house over there? I had it built to resemble a Mississippi Delta sharecropper's house. Do you know who lives there, Mr. Jensen? *I* do every once in a while."

"Huh?"

"Yes, I have to. You see, Mr. Jensen, I do not have much experience at the hard work that Quincy did in the Delta. He slaved there for so long that playing the blues is like second nature for him. Not so with me.

"Every once in a while, when it looks like I cannot play the way I would like to, or the songs I write do not seem to come together just right, I know the problem. It is because I have had it too easy. My best songs that Midnight plays are usually written after I have spent awhile in that old house, living the way I did with Quincy, in Rosedale. It requires extraordinary discipline. Louise, Rose, and Quincy stay here and leave me to myself. But I try to live out the life of a sharecropper. I do not know if I will *ever* get to the point I no longer feel the need to do that, Mr. Jensen. One has to make sacrifices. This is mine."

"Mistah Jensen?" Quincy interjected. "Wud you lack tah see how's tah make a fife?"

"Why, certainly!" Roger exclaimed.

"Ah-ite, let's go down tah dah uthah house." Rose, Louise, Ian, and Roger walked with Quincy to the sharecropper's house.

"Maybe seeing the inside will help you visualize what it is like inside a Mississippi Delta sharecropper's house," Louise said.

"I suppose so," Roger commented, as he stared about the one-room shanty with inquisitive eyes. His eyes first rested on the wood stove, and he noticed the exhaust pipe that ran upward through the ceiling.

"I hab's tah hab dis cane shipt tah me all dah way frum dah Delta bot'mland e'bry yeah," Quincy told Roger. "Can't fine it ovuh heah. Fust, you gotsta' git a good, hot fi-ah goin' in dah stove."

"And, yes, Quincy's wood stove was shipped in, too," Rose interrupted. "That's why it looks so old, cause it *is* old."

"Ra-at, sho' did," Quincy added. "I fust gotsta' hab a knife I kin han'l real good. Then I staht strippin' dah cane, while my pokuh in dah stove, it be gittin' hot. Whin dah pokuh real good an' hot, I put dah cane on dah flo'. Din I holds' it wid my feets."

"Mr. Jensen, did you understand all that Quincy just said?" Ian asked with a jeer.

"Not really, but that's all right; keep going. I'll figure it out or else ask."

Quincy began burning holes in the cane where his fingers would eventually fit.

"How do you know exactly where to put the holes? I mean, does it matter?"

"Oh yes," Ian volunteered, "it matters. But Quincy doesn't need a measuring tool. He can just look at it and tell where to put the holes. That can't be taught, Mr. Jensen. It's a gift."

"Yep," Quincy said. "Bin doin' it so lone, it ain't dat hahd tah tell weah tah buhn dah holes. I ahways spit on dah place dat I want tah buhn dah next hole." Quincy occasionally put the cane up to his lips tah get thuh right feel o' thuh fife. "Din, aftuh you buhn dese six holes, you staht on dah mouth end an' buhn through dah cane, tah make it hollah'."

Quincy blew off all the excess shavings and then hummed a tune to himself. Next, he played the fife to see if it matched his hum. "Dis is how's I toon it. I haves tah hum fust."

Before long, Quincy was entertaining the other four with his freshly-made instrument. They had front row seats that many blues fans would have paid dearly for. Roger Jensen had already begun to understand why Ian had asked Quincy to move to England. Ian knew there would come a day when Quincy would be too old to take care of himself. What better way to repay Quincy than to take care of him? Besides, Quincy had no savings or Social Security supplement to fall back on. Mr. Morganson had never withheld Social Security taxes on the laborers. Sometimes, he didn't pay them in cash, but in those small, stamp-like pieces of paper they called scrip.

Roger had to know. "Mr. Quarles?"

"Yeah."

"Would you play something with Midnight?"

"It's no use," Ian intervened. "I have asked him to play with us on many occasions. But he is not going to face a crowd here, nor would he in his Delta homeland."

"What if I could assure you, Quincy, that there will be no ghosts?" Roger asked.

Quincy remained silent for a moment. Then he asked, "All my life I bin tole if'n I git 'roun' big crowds, ghosts gone cum. How can *you* a-shuah me o' no ghosts?"

Roger answered, "Well, I've always heard—at least in England—that if you kill a raven and then hang him in a beech tree, you will get rid of your ghosts. Do not take him down until the next full moon. Ghosts detest dead ravens."

"What be's a raven?"

Ian said, "Oh that's right. Quincy, Mr. Jensen means a crow. The raven looks something like a crow. I guess you could say, Quincy, this is the Englishman's reh-muh-dee for fear of ghosts."

Quincy hesitated, then he replied, "Sho' 'nuff? Dat keep 'way ghosts?"

Roger answered, "It has always worked here in England."

Quincy was still somewhat reluctant.

Before Quincy could answer, Rose interrupted. "Quincy, I've never asked you to do anything for me, have I?"

"Cum tah thank of it, I reckon' not, guhl."

"Well, I am now. I would like for you to try it."

The room grew very quiet. Ian knew Quincy well enough to know when he was pondering. Rose and Louise also knew it was best not to speak. Even Roger sensed that he should cease his interview for a moment while Quincy thought through the situation.

Eighteen

National Stadium, Stockholm
Two months later

  HELIX, MIDNIGHT'S FRONT BAND, played before eighty thousand cheering rock and roll fans. It was Midnight's opening night, and it had been more than a year since their last tour. Backstage, the band was getting prepared to go on.
  "Well, this is it," Louise said to Ian. "Midnight will do well."
  Rose smiled and nodded in agreement. Ian turned to look over his shoulder. "Quincy, are you ready?"
  "Yep," Quincy said, putting out his cigarette, "I reckon' so."
  "Okay, don't forget," Ian advised, "look for the raven. I mean, crow. Look for the crow in the tree."
  Helix was playing their last song. The crowd was getting wilder by the moment, and the audience seemed to sense Midnight was due to come out soon. Back stage stood Roger Jensen, pen and paper in hand. Quincy peeked around the corner to view the crowd--the crowd that he had always feared. He knew that Midnight had played for years before such crowds. Quincy had never had the desire to go with Midnight on tour, preferring to stay at the castle, for he had always been taught that his fear of ghosts could not be conquered.
  The time came for Helix to exit.
  "Good evening!" Ian exclaimed to the ecstatic crowd.
  Midnight played for the next two hours without a break. When the crowd cried out for more, Ian looked back at Peter, Colin, and Niles. Peering off stage, Ian spotted Rose and Louise. All five of them seemed to be enjoying the night. Quincy had always loved playing for small audiences. But he had never had to deal with ghosts. Thinking about it only increased Quincy's apprehension. "I gotsta' keeps my eyes on dat raven," he said to himself.
  "Thank you, thank you very much," said Ian. "Some of you have been fans of Midnight for ten years now. For that, Peter, Colin, Niles, and I say thank you."
  The loud and rambunctious crowd settled down and listened to Ian's speech. They were not accustomed to hearing any of Midnight's members speak before or after a concert. Off to the side, Roger Jensen was listening intently.

"Normally," Ian began, "we just play our hit songs and perhaps two or three new ones to promote our next album. However, tonight is different. We have a special guest star with us tonight. Few of you have ever heard of him, I'm quite certain. He hails from the United States. No, he's not the next Jimi Hendrix. In fact, he isn't anything of the sort. I met him years ago in the Deep South of America. He's not like your average rock and roll star. In fact, he doesn't claim to be, or pursue the career of, a rock star. Before there was a British music invasion in America, there were the black blues players, playing in obscurity to their indigenous communities of the Deep South.

"I am here to tell you that no one has influenced my music the way this man has. Every rock and roll band owes it all to blues players like this man. Were it not for these men and women, rock and roll would never have existed, for rock and roll is based from the blues music like you will hear in a few minutes. Midnight would not be where it is today if it were not for this man's countless contributions. He is my mentor. Ladies and gentlemen, I have talked enough. I give you Quincy Quarles."

The majority of the Swedish crowd did not understand most of what Ian said. But they seemed to sense something spectacular was about to happen, so they began to cheer. Reluctantly, Quincy made his way on stage, with harmonica in pocket and acoustic guitar in hand. He was wearing a black suit with a narrow black polyester tie. The tie was secured by a gold-plated clasp, fastened to his new white dress shirt. His pants were held up by his favorite pair of galluses.

Ian had set a stool out front for his mentor. At the back of the stadium stood a twenty-foot tall beech tree. Ian had arranged for roadies to prop the tree in clear view of the stage. That was of utmost importance. And in the beech hung a mounted black raven. Quincy had already located the bird when he was backstage. He seemed to have settled down.

"Hello, ladies and gentlemen," he said, with a Lucky Strike dangling from his mouth. Quincy slowly put out the cigarette with his shoe. Propping his left leg onto the highest rung of the barstool, Quincy then placed his guitar onto his leg. The crowd was anxiously silent. Midnight's members had rehearsed with Quincy and knew when to accompany Quincy and when to let him play solo.

> *Cone bread an' puhpil huhs,*
> *I said, Cone bread an' puhpil huhs,*
> *Dat be all I know to eat,*
> *I said, Dat be all I know tah eat.*
>
> *Hahd times an' mo' hahd times,*
> *I said, Hahd times an' mo' hahd times,*
> *Dat be alls I know*
> *Dat be alls I know.*

Ian gave the nod, and the band chimed in, bringing the crowd to its feet. Never had Sweden or the rest of Europe witnessed an old black man on an acoustic guitar, leading England's--and perhaps the continent's--greatest rock and roll band. Occasionally, Quincy played his harmonica--the same ten-cent one he had been playing for fifty years or more.

Two roadies quickly carried Quincy's quills and fife out to the front. Quincy would intersperse the guitar playing with his quills or fife. It did not seem to make any difference what Quincy did, whether he sang or played, or both; the crowd could not get enough. From the piano bench, Ian frequently gave a glance to Louise, Rose, and Roger. Roger returned the nod. Roger felt just as the crowd, mesmerized by one of the greatest blues players in history. He had put away his pen and paper, deciding to enjoy the unprecedented moment. He also realized that this should increase his magazine subscriptions greatly, which was what Mick wanted, anyway.

Quincy and Midnight played for an hour and a half. Ian's mentor was now seventy-five years old, and Ian did not want him to overdo it. Yet, Quincy seemed to be enjoying the playing and the crowd as much as anyone. Ian came and stood by him, giving him a hug and a great big smile.

"Quincy Quarles, ladies and gentleman, one of the greatest blues players—ever!" exclaimed a jubilant Ian Smythe. The crowd seemed delirious, demanding an encore. Quincy and Midnight obliged them—twice. Then, Ian walked to the microphone. "That's it, ladies and gentlemen. You've been a very gracious crowd to us tonight. Thank you. Good night." Quincy did a small bow, as did all of Midnight's members.

Everyone backstage was also applauding, including Roger Jensen. No one thought it would go over this well. Rose was the first to greet Quincy backstage. "Well, you did it, Quincy! You conquered your fear of ghosts, *and* you were a sensation with this young crowd! Congratulations!"

All of Midnight's members and Louise were there to congratulate Quincy.

"Don't be giv'n me all dah credit. You boy-ahs did a good job, too. Y'all pritty good yo'self, don't forgit. Most ah all, thank dah Lawd I con-quhd my fear ah ghosts jest by keepin' my eyes peeled on dat ol' crow—o' raven, whatevah he be."

For the next two months, Midnight, Helix, and Quincy toured Europe. They were an instant hit in all of Europe. Concerts were sold out as soon as the tickets went on sale. Sales of Midnight's previous albums tripled. Even Helix's two albums were hard to find in music stores. Newspapers in the States were covering the tour as well. But Ian had made Roger Jensen give his word that he could never tell where Quincy

Quarles was discovered. All Ian ever said from the stage was that Quincy was from the Deep South, as Quincy had requested.

Rock and roll fans desperately wanted to find Quincy's albums. Little did they know at the time that there were none to be bought--at any price. While in Mississippi, Ian kept the recording equipment in the back of his rented car, but he never had anywhere to plug it in. And barrelhouses never held the equipment to record, either.

Since Quincy had been living in England, he had continued—by choice—to live the life of a recluse. It was Quincy's idea to become the butler. He did not care about being discovered; he just wanted to live out his life in seclusion.

Just after completing the European tour, Midnight's members returned to their own respective homes in and around the Cambridge area. Niles owned a villa in Geneva, but for the most part, he, as well as the other band's members, preferred to stay near Cambridge. They were not a typical band, nor did they try to be. They were unpredictable. It was due to Quincy's influence. He had not only made an impression on Ian, Louise, Roger, and Rose; in different ways, Quincy Quarles had unintentionally touched almost all of the Englishmen with whom he had contact. That's just the way it was with the old blues players. They did not put on airs; they merely wrote blues and played them because that was what they knew how to do.

NOT LONG AFTER returning to the castle from their European tour, Quincy accosted Ian in the parlor.

"You know what I's fixin' to say, don't you?"

"I think I do. You want to return to the Delta, don't you?"

"Yep."

"For good?"

"Yep. I reckon' so. You know whud dey say, all good thangs must cum tah an end."

"I have dreaded this day, but I felt it coming. I can't blame you, Quincy. England is different from the way you were brought up."

"Yep, sho' is. You only stayed in dah Delta fo' two munths. I bin heah dah bettah paht o' fo'teen ye-ahs. In meny ways, it's bin good heah. I sho' wuldn't git dis treatment weah I's cum frum. Rose taught me how's tah read 'n write. I dun libbed in dis cassel. I watcht Rose grow up. Meny thangs heah bin good. Can't cumplain." Quincy paused. "But it ain't home. I can't 'xplain it. Eb'n do' thangs ain't jest ra-at wid blacks an' whites deah in dah Delta, it's all I evah knowd till I stay heah. I don't know how dem blues playuhs who moved off tah Shee-cah-go an' Deetroit deal wid it. I reckon' paht of it coul' also be dats wheah my wife an' son be buh-eed back deah.

"You know, Dovie Ruth an' Lena both died since I bin heah. Den, Quo-tez pass 'way. My friend Luthah Ray is still 'roun', but he old, too. I reckon' I awt tah spen my last days back weah's I wuz bone. Dat's jest dah way it is."

"I couldn't agree more. You know that you are welcome to stay here as long as you like. But I want what you want. If you feel it's time to return, I will respect that. But *you* are going to have to break the news to Louise and Rose."

"Yep, I thought you might say dat. But it's ah-ite. I'll tell 'em."

"When would you like to go back?"

"I reckon a week o' so, if'n you 'el hep me arrange dah flight an' git a holda' Lena's son, Hank. He kin git me at dah Memphis aihpote. Thangs lack dat."

"Will do. Anything you need, you know all you have to do is ask."

"Pree-shee-ate it. You bin awful good to me, Ian. Dun paid me tah do dis heah easy job at butlerin'. Paid me tah go on too-ah wid you. Thangs lack dat. I gots 'nuff money tah live on dah rest ah my life. Who knows? Maybe dah ol' house I wuz stayin' in whin you foun' me fo'teen ye-ahs ago is still standin'. Wouln't mine libbin' deah again."

Nineteen

Rosedale, Mississippi—July of that same year

IT WAS TEN O'CLOCK in the evening at Quincy's old house. No one had lived there since Quincy, fourteen years earlier. Out of sheer neglect, the house was falling in. Seventy-five-year-old Quincy sat on the porch, playing the ten-cent harmonica he bought when he was nineteen. His playing was interspersed with singing, while he also held a Lucky Strike at the corner of his mouth. His recent popularity in Europe and the States, to a degree, made him appreciate the backwoods solitude even more.

But then, something went wrong. Quincy slumped over. Right then and there on the levee bosses' old house, Quincy Quarles' heart quit beating while he remained upright in his favorite straight-back chair. It would be two days before Luther Ray, Quincy's friend of sixty-five years, would find him.

News traveled quickly in the States and to other continents. Within two hours of finding Quincy Quarles, Ian was notified in Cambridge of his death. Louise, Rose, Ian, Peter, Colin, and Niles arranged for their Concorde flight to JFK International, the new name for New York International Airport. When the group arrived in Memphis on their charted Cessna 414, Ian observed that Memphis' airport had also changed its name from Memphis Municipal Airport to Memphis International Airport. Roger Jensen also had heard of Quincy's death and asked Ian if he might accompany them. Ian felt it would be appropriate--so much so that he even paid for his expensive airfare. Roger was instrumental in coaxing Quincy to go on tour with Midnight. Ian had made millions over the last ten years playing in Britain's greatest rock and roll band. Although Ian was usually frugal, time was of the essence; and this was no time to pinch pennies. From there, a limousine escorted them to Rosedale.

The British entourage—all of them donning long hair and odd attire--drove into Rosedale late the next afternoon. They soon discovered that Lena's children were handling funeral arrangements at Rimsey's Funeral Home of Rosedale. It was the only black funeral home within eighty miles. Ian and the group eventually found the funeral home. Upon entering, they quickly observed the number of visitors who had come to pay their respects. There was standing room only. Louise recognized one of Lena's children.

"Hassie?" asked Louise, as she began to make her way over to Lena's oldest daughter.

"Hey, guhl!" exclaimed Hassie, smiling. "Good to see ya'. Bin a lone' time, ain't it."

"Too long. Did you ever meet Ian, my husband?"

"No. I remembah heahin' 'bouts 'eem plenty, do'. Who be dis?"

"This is Rose, our daughter. And these others, well, that's Niles over there, this is Colin, and Peter, well, I don't see him. He must have gone to the restroom. This is Roger Jensen, a magazine reporter—and friend."

A moment later, a black man in a three-piece suit interrupted their reminiscing. "Hassie, I am Doctah Alfred Moore. I'm pastuh of Ebenezer Greater Missionary Bab-tis Chuch, in Winstonville. Mr. Rimsey called me an' axsed if I'd ah-fish-ee-ate dah foo-ner-uhl. Since I knowd meny o' Quincy's fam'ly, I tole 'em I'd do it."

Mr. Rimsey recognized Hassie and approached her. "I have a will in my hand, if you want to call it dat. Kin sum o' yo' fam'ly membuhs sit down wid me, an' let's go ovah it in my office?"

"Sho'," said Hassie. "Ian an' Louise, you may as well cum, too. I don't thank Uncle Quincy had much whin he left heah. We didn't keep in touch as much as we prob'ly should hab. So, whatevuh he has, he prob'ly left it tah uthahs."

Dr. Moore, Ian, Louise, Rose, and Hassie sat down and listened as Mr. Rimsey read the will.

"I'm gone read yo' Mistah Quoles' will like he wrote it. He left dis note in the levee bosses' house: 'I don't thank I hab lone to live. Bin coffin' a lots lately. Should anybody fine dis note, I hab sum requests. One, I ask to be bureed up et Waxhaw, next to my wife and son. I hab a few valu-bels that I leave certen peoples. I leave my harmonica to Peter. If he can't make it to my foon-eral, pleas see if you kin git it to him. My fife, it goes to Colin. And my guitar, well, it can go to Niles. Rose kin have my quills cause she wuz always fassinated by them. She taught me how to read and write. Ain't her fault if'n I misspell anythang. Oh yeah, my twelve-gauge shotgun and fav-uh-it pair of overalls, give them to Luther Ray. Seem like he never culd scrounj up 'nuff money to buy hisself a gun.

"Two things I been wantin over the last few years. One is a reel to reel tape machine like the one Ian brought up here fourteen years ago. In England I watched them to see how to ah-pah-rate it. The other thang I always wantid was to spend the night in a house in these parts that hads elektrisity. I made nuff money in England to have the uteelty boys stretch a power line over here several months back. So to Louise and Ian, who asked their daughter Rose to teach me to read and write, I give my songs. All six hunded and fifteen of them I wrot down to the best of my memory. They in a safe deposit box at Rosedale Unyon Bank. You will also find reel to reel tapes of all these songs. Ain't nobody on them tapes but me. Sorry I didn't have no band to back me up. But I know y'all recoded us on that Eurup tour, anyways. I sang all of them ovuh the last few months on this front porch. They be for Ian and Louise.

"I ain't afraid of dying. I know where I be going. I'm gone see if me an' Jesus kin strike up a blues song togethah, but I dout there be much blues up there in heaven. I was bone and raised in these parts. I seen lots of black men suffah. But I have no regrets. 'Cause if I hadn' had dah blues all these years, I wouldn' know how to teach Ian or nobody else. I hold no grudges toward any man. I have learned grudges toward any man don't help atall. Love. Quincy Quarles'."

"Well, I kin say dat I'm glad he wuz my uncle," Hassie said. "'Bout month ago, Uncle Quincy had me cum visit 'eem. I reckon' he sensed sumpin' was wrong wid 'eem. He tole me tah fine' enythang in dat little house I wanted, 'ceptin' o' cose dem thangs dat Mistah Rimsey jest read off. I gots a few thangs. Uncle Quincy, he a good man. Fo-chu-naht-lee, he died wheah he wanted tah, ra-at deah on dat po'ch, his fa-vuh-ite spot on uhth."

Dr. Moore and Mr. Rimsey nodded in agreement while the British visitors just listened. Tears began to develop in the eyes of all the British visitors, even Roger's.

Visitors continued to enter and pay their respects. Happy, Jeremiah, Percy, Slim Willie, and Luther Ray were all there. The time finally came for the funeral service to begin.

Before Dr. Moore began his sermon, a woman whom Ian did not immediately recognize stood and came to the lectern. She wore a black satin dress. "Hello, ladies and gentlemen," she said. Once Ian heard her voice, he knew instantly that it was Inez Jefferson. He had not seen her in more than fourteen years. "Yeahs ago, Quincy had axsed me tah sing dis song at his foo-ner-al. He said dat when he was a jackleg preacher many yeahs ago, dey sang dis in chh-uch. He said no song touched him more dan dis one wrote by Miss F. W. Suffield. Please pray fo' me as I sing."

In the harvest field now ripened,
There's work for all to do;
Hark, the voice of God is calling,
To the harvest calling you.
Little is much when God is in it,
Labor not for wealth or fame;
There's a crown and you can win it,
If you go in Jesus' name.
Does the place you're called to labor
Seem so small and little known?
It is great if God is in it,
And He'll not forget His own.

> *Little is much when God is in it,*
> *Labor not for wealth or fame;*
> *There's a crown and you can win it,*
> *If you go in Jesus' name.*
> *When the conflict here is ended*
> *And our race on earth is run,*
> *He will say, if we are faithful,*
> *"Welcome home, my child, well done."*
> *Little is much when God is in it,*
> *Labor not for wealth or fame;*
> *There's a crown and you can win it,*
> *If you go in Jesus' name.*

Ian and family, Roger, Colin, Niles, and Peter sat over to one side. They had hoped that no other reporters other than Roger would show up. However, a *Jackson Daily News* reporter from Mississippi's capital city came late and stood near the front door, since there was standing room only.

Dr. Moore stood to deliver his sermon. "Just as Quincy left wuhd fo' Miss Jeffuhsun to sing at his foo-ner-al, he also left wuhd whut Bible vus he want used at his foo-ner-al. It cums frum dah Gospel o' John, dah sixth chaptuh. In dah ninth vus, Andrew said to *Je*-sus, 'Deah is a lad here, which ha' fi' bahley loaves, and two small fishes: but whut are they among so many?' Hassie, Quincy's niece, tole me dah utha day when we got wuhd Quincy die, dat his favuhit vus was dis vus. It definitely go wid dat song Miss Jeffuhsun sang."

Amen's were frequently shouted here and there. One woman yelled in ecstasy, "Praise dah Lawd, Quincy bin dee-liv-uhd." All of the Britishmen listened respectfully, but didn't know what to make of the woman chanting deliriously, or the cacophony of Amen's.

"Fo' sho', Quincy had little growing up in this Delta," Dr. Moore continued. "As mose of you know, Quincy move to Englan' some yeahs back. He began to have money then. I huhd he eb'n lived in a manshun ovuh deah. I's heah to tell ya', Quincy in a biggah manshun tee-day. I huhd also Quincy kepts a gahdin ovuh deah in Englun', too. I know he's in a bettuh gahdin tee-day."

"Amen! Preach on, Rev!"

"But eb'n when Quincy growin' up heah in dah Delta, he was content wid whut he had," Dr. Moore continued. "He nevah tried to git mo' dan he needed. He gave away any extra he evuh had."

Dr. Moore preached for another twenty minutes. Finally, it was time for the pallbearers to carry Quincy to the hearse and on to the cemetery. The sun was settling down in the horizon as the entourage followed Mr. Rimsey's black hearse to the Waxhaw Cemetery.

Standing next to the casket, Dr. Moore spoke a few last words. "Bruthahs an' sistahs heah t'day, let me say that it was good fo' you tah cum out an' show support fo' this man, Quincy Quolz. Main thang, he knew *Je*-sus as his Savyah. Quincy, well, he played in dem honky-tonks for yeahs. But even still, Jesus fo'gave 'eem an' save 'eem. Now, Quincy be in heaven. Dat's whut dah Bible say."

Several onlookers shouted "Amen" to Dr. Moore's gravesite eulogy. Others simply nodded.

Hassie's sons and brothers assisted Mr. Rimsey in laying Quincy's casket into the ground. Quincy had specified to Hassie that he was to be buried in a plain pine casket, for that was all in which he could bury his wife and son. Midnight's members, Louise, Rose, and many of Quincy's Delta friends softly placed their lapel roses on the top of the casket. Of those from Britain, only Louise was accustomed to the July heat and humidity. Ian had almost forgotten what it was like, and his British comrades and his daughter Rose had never experienced such a miserable climate. It was a good thing that at the Memphis airport, Louise had wisely suggested that they buy some handkerchiefs.

"Well, Doctah Mo', dat wuz as beu-tee-ful a suh-vis as I evuh bin to," Hassie said.

Dr. Moore just smiled as if he were a bit proud of his eloquence.
"Louise, hab ya' huhd 'bout yo' folks' place?" Hassie asked.
"No. What?"

"Dat ol' mean man Hawkins. Aftuh he bought dah place from you, he set 'bout makin' thangs hahdeh fo' all us black folk. Jest like dah new Pharaoh dun in Egypt 'bout Moses' time. Yo' daddy was tin times bettah tah us dan dis man. Mean ol' snake, he is. Suhvs 'eem ra-at, too."

"What do you mean by serves him right?" asked Louise.

"You ain't huhd, is ya'? Mr. Hawkins is gone broke. He invested sum o' his money in dah awl fiel's in 'nutha country. An' dey's habb'n an' awl crisus deah. It make 'eem go undah. Now he's gotsta' sell yo' ol' place—all o' it—just tah pay his bills."

"No, I hadn't heard. But wait a minute! What will all of you workers do?"

"Don't know jest yet. Mistah Hawkins dun fah wuhse dan all dem yeahs yo' folks hab dah place. I wish it wuz lack useta' be."

Louise glanced at Ian, only to discover that he was already looking her way. But neither said a word as the crowd dismissed. Everyone but the British entourage and Hassie had left.

"Are you thinking what I'm thinking?" Louise asked her husband.

Twenty

The Old Morganson Plantation—two months later

LOUISE, ROSE, AND IAN were sitting on the back porch where Louise had grown up.

"Ian," said Louise, "You don't have any regrets, do you?"

"No, of course not."

"I'm certainly glad y'all returned," remarked Freddie Lou. "It's been a long time since I got to be with my best friend, Louise." Freddie Lou was now married, with two girls of her own, but she had not gained any weight as many of the Southern belles did once they settled down into a marriage. The two women embraced again.

"I'm so glad you bought this place back, Mama," Rose said.

"So are we, Dear. So are we."

"Midnight can continue without me," Ian said. "I was just the fortunate one who came here fifteen years ago to meet Quincy, and of course, to meet you."

"Hey, Mistah Smythe, weah does yo' want dis heah trailuh put fo' dah night?" Luther Ray asked.

"Right there is fine, Luther Ray. But you know, it's Ian, and not Mistah Smythe."

"Ah-ite. Cott'n sho' is stahtin' tah look real good. An' it fo *sho'* is good wuckin' fo' y'all. I kin say dat fo' sho'. Ain't no white boss evuh bin dis good dat I kin recall. No aw-fence, Miss Louise."

"I agree," Louise said.

"The only way I can maintain the ability to play blues music is if I help *y'all* in *dah fiels*," Ian added with a chuckle. Then he added, "You know what they say, you gotta' hab thah blues tah sang thah blues."

"Dat ain't bad dah way you tryin' tah copy us black folk," Luther Ray commented.

"Yep," Ian remarked as he continued adapting his words to the jargon of the South, "only one thang wrong. Quincy *ain't heah tah heah me.*"

The End